STARRING Minnie Piper

The LADYBIRD Code

D0260256

To Tony Oakhill, a shining star, thank you.
~ C J

To Lauren
~ K L

STRIPES PUBLISHING
An imprint of Magi Publications
1 The Coda Centre, 189 Munster Road, London SW6 6AW

A paperback original
First published in Great Britain in 2007

Text copyright © Caroline Juskus, 2007
Illustrations copyright © Kate Leake, 2007

ISBN-13: 978-1-84715-021-9

A CIP catalogue record for this book is available from the British Library.

Printed in Belgium by Proost

2 4 6 8 10 9 7 5 3 1

STARRING

Minnie Piper

The LADYBIRD Code

Caroline Juskus

Illustrated by
Kate Leake

Stripes

It is mind-bogglingly Peculiar

that the 'missing' letters in this message

will explain why I went to bed on

Monday night ☺.

and everything wa_ totally normal and

yawningly boring and wh_n I woke up

10 hours later, before I _ould say,

"Four days to my Best Pa_ty ever!"

th_ strangest _hings

were _tarting to happen!

(you can doodle your answer here)

buzz

This is my puzzling party invite!

You are invited to Minnie's
TOP-Secret Birthday Party
And this is your 1st Secret CLUE!!
19th HOUR 12th DAY, 10th MONTH
Tell no one and all will be revealed.
More clues coming soon!

I handed it out yesterday, and all my friends are secretly excited but ... I'm not the only one sending out puzzles because this has just arrived in the post! It is handmade and someone has cut out two pink hearts and glued them together about the edges to make an envelope. And it is totally peculiar because I never get post, except on my birthday (which is next Monday). But I'm not supposed to save it till then because this is what it says on the back...

Minnie Piper
Flat 53, Block B
Arthurs Way
Hill Tops

OPEN TUESDAY!

And very excitingly, today is Tuesday! I tear the envelope open and I cannot believe it, but inside is a sheet of tissue and this is what it says:

Minnie, here's a riddle
That's my birthday gift to you
Puzzle very carefully
And you will
SPOT THE CLUE!

"What does that mean?!" I gasp, showing it to Dad.

"Perhaps it's a secret LOVE letter!" he laughs. "It is heart-shaped, after all!"

"And you have to work out who it's from," giggles Mum. "I never knew you had an admirer!"

And I immediately blush because I have never had a LOVE letter before, but before I can take another peep Dad looks at his watch and panics,

"You only have three minutes to catch the school bus, Minnie!"

And this is no-time-for-reading annoying, and I have to stuff the riddle into my pocket and leg it to the corner of Arthurs Way. I get there three seconds before the bus, but this is perfect because Trevor and Tiffany are waiting too and more than three seconds with the Terrible T's is definitely too much!

I've been desperate to catch the bus for weeks, because then I can go to school with Frankie, and

now Mum has had to agree as, after zillions of hints, she's finally making me a new bedroom. She's got a week off work and wants to decorate it ASAP so it's out of the way before my birthday. Then she can concentrate on my top-secret party! And all this means she's **HUMUNGOUSLY** busy and has no time for morning walks!

Frankie is saving me a seat and it's my turn to sit by the window because it was her turn yesterday. It's the best seat because you can huff on the window and write secret messages which *disappear* until you huff on them again. But right now I have my own secret message, burning a hole in my coat pocket, and I'm about to tell Frankie when...

"Are you going to give me another Party Clue?" she grins.

"Maybe!" I tell her. "But first I need to show you..."

"I can't wait to see it. Is it purple again?"

"Of course," I grin, "it's my favourite colour!" And to keep her happy I sneakily pass her...

Minnie's TOP-Secret Birthday Party
This is your 2nd Secret CLUE –
IT WILL BE BEHIND THE RED DOORS
IN THE HALL WALLS
LOTS of room for LOTS of F.U.N
Next clue coming soon!

"Fabiozo!" she giggles. "It's going to be the best party ever."

"I know," I tell her, "and you'll never believe it but…" and I've nearly told her I'm getting a DJ, when Tiffany Me-Me sits right behind us. This is trying-to-scratch-your-back annoying as I do not want Tiff to overhear. My riddle and party are both secret and me and Frankie have been thinking party thoughts for two weeks and Frankie's very first thought was DO NOT INVITE TREVOR OR TIFFANY! She's even made me a best-party list…

HOW TO MAKE MINNIE'S PARTY FABAROONY

a) do NOT invite Trevor or Tiffany
b) invite lots of cool people
c) get a disco with a real DJ
d) wish for a bubble machine and dry ice
e) give the party a theme
f) lots of cool decorations
g) yummy food
h) must NOT be squashed in Minnie's flat

Frankie says the first point is extra important because Trevor would pick his nose (and the crisps) and Tiffany would be in charge of everything and it would be especially awful instead of specially brilliant. But this means I have to be mind-bogglingly clever if I am ever going to get to Saturday without them finding out. So I huff on the window and doodle

Tiffany sees it and says, "Do you love Daniel Jackman, Minnie?"

"No!" I tell her.

"Then why have you written his initials on the window?"

"I haven't," I sigh.

"Have!" says Tiff. And she totters off to tell the entire bus I love the drippiest boy on the whole of the planet.

Frankie knows I do NOT love Daniel Jackman but whispers, "Kevin Little will be jealous, Minnie. You know he's got a crush on you!" And my cheeks go HOT because secretly I quite like Kevin. But I am suddenly panicking, what if my riddle IS a LOVE letter ... and it's actually from him?!

I decide I must tell Frankie about my riddle NOW! And I have just whispered, "Frankie, guess what?" when ... GUESS WHAT? The driver tells Trevor to sit down and, as Tiff's still busy spreading rumours, he lollops behind me in her empty seat.

He has a missed-his-mouth cornflake stuck to his chin that wiggles as he grunts, "Wot you up to, Piper?"

I cross my fingers and say, "Actually, I am thinking it might be nice to have sprouts for breakfast."

And he glares at me as if I am mad and says, "You're mental, Piper. Nobody 'as sprouts for breakfast."

"My dad does," I tell him, fingers still crossed. "He has Brussels sprouts on marmalade on toast."

And the thought of eating something green is enough to turn Trevor's stomach and he disappears to the back seats to squeeze in with Abhi and Jasen.

"Yuck!" cringes Frankie.

"What?" I sigh. "Sprouts or Trevor?!"

"Trevor," giggles Frankie. "And does DJ mean you're getting a DJ, Minnie?"

"Plus dry ice and a bubble machine!"

"Foobaroony!"

"I know! My first real party ever!"

"Let's count how many hours till it happens."

"OK," I grin. And we do our sums and $+$ mathematically-brilliantly it is only 106 and five minutes! $\div$ $-$

But my bus trip is annoyingly much shorter and we have got to school before I can tell Frankie about my riddle.

TUESDAY AT SCHOOL

Mr Impey is in his Tuesday-yellow tracksuit, and he's doing star jumps in front of the board and his skinny plaits are flying about like dizzy black worms.

"Class Chickenpox," he beams, "who wants to hear some exciting news?"

We all ignore him because Trevor has tied Jasen's trainers to his chair legs and everyone is watching and Tiffany Me-Me is bossily tutting. But Mr Impey keeps jumping up and down and counts, "Star jump one … star jump two…". And when he has jumped one hundred and forty-nine times we are all finally ready.

"149 seconds," he sighs. "Tomorrow there will be one more marble for your marble pot if you can be quiet quicker, but one marble less if you can't!"

"Can we exclude Trevor?" groans Tiffany.

"No," says Mr Impey. "We are all a team and we must all learn to work together."

And this is what I hate about school – being in teams with Tiffany and Trevor. And I completely forget Mr Impey has exciting news until he shouts, "SO AS I WAS SAYING, TODAY I HAVE EXCITING NEWS!!"

"Is school cancelled then?" heckles Trevor.

"No," says Mr Impey.

"Are we having non-uniform day?" asks Tiffany.

"No," says Mr Impey, "it isn't that."

"Can we bring our pets into school?" ask Delilah and Tallulah. And they probably have identical goldfish because they are can't-tell-the-difference identical twins.

"No," sighs Mr Impey. And this is a shame as I could have brought my dog, Wanda Wellingtons, as I'm already teaching her MORSE code (which is this week's topic for World War Two) and she would probably have known more than Trevor!

Frankie asks if we're doing a 'STARS in their EYES' show, and when Mr Impey says, "No," I'm can't-sing-or-dance relieved as I would rather *spell* YODELLING XYLOXPHONIST than actually *be* one.

But if it isn't this, I cannot imagine what it can be and I am thinking teachers always SAY things are exciting, but usually they are NOT.

And when we have run out of good ideas Mr Impey says, "I could just tell you," and we sigh, "OK," and know it's going to be bad.

Mr Impey calls Delilah and Tallulah up to the front and says, "How do you like being twins, girls?"

Delilah giggles, and I know it's Delilah because I can see her purple hair bobble, and Delilah's hair bobble is always purple and Tallulah's is always pink. And Tallulah says, "It's fun being a twin because we both know what each other's thinking."

And I'm thinking, Frankie and I always know what each other's thinking so maybe she's my secret twin and she's thinking about my

TREVOR SMELLS

PHEWWW!

peculiar riddle. But before I can check Mr Impey says, "Well, good news, Chickenpoxers, you're all about to be twins!"

And I am sure this is biologically not actually possible when he adds, "We're being twinned with a school in Australia! You're going to get Australian penfriends and learn about their life down under – their weather, their wildlife, and what it's like to go to school on the other side of the world. You'll be emailing each other with all your news and sending a photo so your penfriends can see what you look like. The photographer will be in school tomorrow and Mr Hooper has requested that you wear full uniform AND have tidy hair. Oh, yes, and for Friday lunch we'll be eating Australian food!"

Uh-oh! I am can't-think-of-anything-to-say useless at emails and I do not like having my photo taken and it's physically IMPOSSIBLE to have tidy hair when it looks like a million spiralling slinkies. Oh yes, and I'm sure I won't like nibbling kangaroo!

"If this is exciting news," grunts Trevor, "I 'ate to think wot bad news would be."

And for the first time in history I think he's right!

TUESDAY AT LUNCH

At lunchtime Frankie and me are behind the pet shed and AT LAST I can tell her about my riddle. I am giddily excited and hopping up and down and Frankie asks, "Do you need the loo, Minnie?"

"No," I tell her, "but I do need to show you something!" And I scrabble in my pocket for my pink-heart envelope and Frankie smiles and says, "Are you writing a 𝕃𝕆𝕍𝔼 letter, Minnie?"

"Course not," I sigh. "It's not FROM me, but TO me."

"Oh, a birthday card. Then you mustn't open it till next Monday or it'll bring you bad luck."

"It isn't a birthday card!" I say. And I turn it over and show her...

OPEN TUESDAY !

"Oh," says Frankie. "Who gave you that?"

"I don't know. It came this morning in the proper post."

"And you didn't tell me?! Has your tongue got tied in a *tanglew* ?"

I stick my tongue out to prove it's fine and say, "I've been itching to tell you all morning, but you and Mr Impey wouldn't stop talking, and I couldn't squeeze in a single word."

"Is it an invite to a garden party?" she giggles, as I take out the riddle and she peeks at the flowers.

"No," I grin. "It's better than that!" And we both read…

Minnie, here's a riddle
That's my birthday gift to you
Puzzle very carefully
And you will
SPOT THE CLUE!

"Foobaroony!" squeals Frankie. "What does it mean?"

"I don't know," I tell her. "But I'm desperate to find out!"

"Can I help?"

"Of course you can, but it's our secret. Don't tell

19

anyone till I know who sent it. I'm worried it might be a 🖤 letter and I don't want Tiffany to find out or she'll tell the whole school."

"Fabiozo," whispers Frankie. "Your first 🖤 letter! Have you got any ideas who sent it?"

"No," I whisper back. "Though it might be…"

But before I can mumble 'Kevin Little' my cling-on cousin Dot arrives and sniffs, "Why are you whispering?"

Dot is nearly half my age and has very nearly half a brain that is totally tuned to bothering me. But, twin-like, Frankie knows what I'm thinking and distracts her with, "Because Grumpy Hooper is letting us adopt school pets and we don't want too many people to know."

I never knew we were allowed to do this (probably because I am scaly-phobic and not into pets with scaly feet or scaly tails as they make my breathing go into a panic), but I say, "We are just thinking what pet we want."

"Oh," sniffs Dot. "Do you want ladybirds, Minnie?"

Irritatingly I realize I'm still holding my riddle and Dot has seen the picture, so I whizz it in my pocket and say, "That's my secret, Dot!"

And Dot says, "Tulip likes secrets. And **ladybirds**. We're doing them in our Mini-Beasts topic, but we don't do adopting them. We're much better at looking after mice."

"Good," says Frankie. "Go and tell Mrs Elliott straight away."

"And don't tell anyone else!" I add.

"OK," sniffs Dot. And she immediately runs off to tell her best friend, Tulip Blackberry Tanner. And Tulip is waving with one hand, and fiddling with her knickers with the other, and she is probably hiding a bag of sweets in them because sweets are banned from being munched in school but Tulip does not stick to rules. And I sigh and say, "Why do all the worst people have names beginning with T?!" And, as quiet as the mouse I'm NOT going to adopt, I add, "NOW shall we try and solve my riddle?"

"OK," giggles Frankie. And we stare at the pictures, but all we can see are roses and violets with bees, ladybirds and butterflies. And it looks fragrantly nice but there's not so much of a whiff of a clue until Frankie squeals, "Roses are red and violets are blue…

Kevin Little MUST LOVE YOU!

And just then Kevin appears behind the pet shed!! And he's not SCALY but my breath quickens as he whispers, "Have you got the next Party Clues, Minnie? Everyone's kind of waiting for them."

"Oh," I mumble. "They're in my bag."

And, whilst I rummage with trembling fingers, I try to peep at him for riddle-making clues, like a

Pritt-**Stick** or scissors sticking out of his pocket. But all I can see is a cute smile and I nearly drop my invitations because he's aiming it at me!

"I'll hand them out if you like," he offers.

"OK," I splutter, "but not to Trevor or Tiffany."

"Cool," he grins.

And I'm sure I'm the colour of strawberry jam, and my hands are definitely just as sticky, and when he has gone, Frankie grins, "I told you, Minnie!"

And I feel kind of faint as the bell goes and I float back to class.

TUESDAY AFTERNOON

All afternoon we study World War Two, which stops me feeling faint and thinking about Kevin because we learn more about **MORSE**. **MORSE** is a mind-bogglingly brilliant way of sending secret messages and it is brain-tinglingly clever because you replace boring letters with dots and dashes. And if someone tries to read your message they cannot know it says SWAP YOU SOME COCOA FOR A PAIR OF GLOVES because dottily it would look like this:

And **MORSE** makes the war a lot more interesting and now it is totally my best topic because puzzling and codes are my speciality. Even when we have to learn about trenches (which is where soldiers lived, and were truthfully, really just muddy ditches that filled up with water and rotted their shoes), it is still fun, because they communicated in MORSE. And when Mr Impey says, "Our friends in Australia were on our side and called our allies," I would usually yawn, but now I want to know all about it because our allies had to tell us things, but secretly so our enemies didn't find out, and so they did it in MORSE.

Yesterday Mr Impey taught us the MORSE alphabet and I copied it down in my Exercise Book and it's a bit tricky and looks like this:

·_ = A   _··· = B   _·_· = C
_·· = D   · = E   ··_· = F
__· = G   ···· = H   ·· = I
·___ = J   _·_ = k   ·_·· = L
__ = M   _· = N   ___ = O
·__· = P   __·_ = Q   ·_· = R
··· = S   _ = T   ··_ = U
···_ = V   ·__ = W   _··_ = X
            _·__ = Y   __·· = Z

And now we each have to write two 6-letter words in **MORSE** and we mustn't let anyone else see, because Mr Impey's going to put them in his empty lunchbox and twizzle them about in his sandwich crumbs. And then we'll pick two each and try to decode them.

This is exactly why Mr Impey is such a whizz teacher and I cannot wait to start doodling.

My first word is   ··· · —·—· ·—· · —

And my second is   ·——· ··— ——·· ——·· ·—·· ·

And cryptically they spell SECRET and PUZZLE which are probably, definitely my two best words. And I cannot see what Frankie is writing because she is being extra, totally, annoyingly

··· · —·—· ·—· · —   and wrapping her arm around her scribblings so I cannot see a thing.

Finally Mr Impey collects our words and puts them in his lunchbox and shakes them about and when it is my turn to select two this is what I pick:

·—· ·· —·· —· ·—·· ·

—·— · ···—· ·· ·—· ·—·

I chose them because they are written in purple and I wish I had thought to do mine like that because it makes them a lot more interesting.

I'm desperate to solve them before anyone else, and instead of waiting to look at Frankie's, I get straight to decoding and so far I have R I D D followed by L E! My word is RIDDLE, which is spine-tinglingly peculiar, especially when my second word, heart-thumpingly, spells KEVIN L!

And I look at Frankie and whisper, "Are these from you?" and I show her my words.

"How can they be?" she grins. "I don't have a purple pen."

"Bet you do!" I whisper. And I grab her pencil case and empty it out, but spookily she is right!

I turn round and peek at Kevin Little, but his head is down and he's busy decoding, and Brainiac Jenny is waving her hand and thinks she's the first to have cracked the codes. And I do not want to say I beat her by a minute, because I do not want to shout out my words. But Jenny is happily shouting hers and they are, "CLEVER TREVOR!"

And everyone laughs because this is something that we never, ever thought we would hear if we lived to be a hundred.

TUESDAY AFTER SCHOOL

99:45.00

At the end of school Frankie calculates that there is now exactly 99 and $^3/_4$ hours till my party. And I decide to start a proper record in the back of my Exercise Book and doodle:

COUNTDOWN TO MINNIE'S BEST PARTY EVER!

Then Frankie crosses her fingers and wishes me luck because I am going back to Gran's for tea and Dot is coming, but not only that, she is bringing her knicker-fiddling, best friend Tulip. Gran is waiting at the school gate and Dot and Tulip are already there, whizzing Spike, my tadpole of a brother, about in his buggy. I smile and pretend I'm pleased to see them but I'm desperate to tell Gran about my riddle. Dot is sniffing, "We're doing  at school, Gran, and me and Tulip have to find facts."

"Oh," says Gran. "I like Mini-Beasts, especially spiders."

"Spiders catch flies in webs," sniffs Dot.

"That's MY fact," says Tulip. "My dad

28

told me and you can't borrow it unless you give me a fact back."

"Oh," sniffs Dot, "but MY dad doesn't know facts."

"Gran does," I tell her. "Gran'll find you one, Dot."

"It has to be very good," says Tulip.

And Gran smiles and says, "I'm sure I've got one tucked up my sleeve." And by the time Dot and Tulip realize there is NOT AN ACTUAL Mini-Beast up Gran's sleeve we are entering Gran's flat.

I ask Gran if I can show her something and she says, "Of course, dear, as soon as I've finished making tea."

And this is entertaining-Dot-and-Tulip too long as Dot is sniffing, "Shall we do drawing a spider, Tulip?" and "Do you want to help, Minnie?" So whilst Gran pops the tea in the oven, Spike plays with leftover pastry and Dot and Tulip and me doodle.

I'm just getting bored when Gran says, "Tea's ready!" and we stare at a quiche and there's a strange spider buried in its middle! Gran has artistically made it with two tomatoes and long green beans and says, "It's a Tuesday 🐛Mini-Beast tea!"

Tulip looks horrified, but Dot claps and counts the legs and sniffs, "Do spiders always have eight legs, Gran?"

"Almost always," smiles Gran, "unless they're magical queen spiders, and in that case they have eleven."

Dot counts the legs of the spider she's drawn and is tarantulally happy when she discovers it's in fact an eleven-legged queen! Tulip hops down from the table and says, "I'm not hungry, thank you very much." And she sounds peculiarly polite, even though she is being rude and stuffing her mouth with a JAMMIE DODGER that was hidden in her pencil case! And, with a pink pen, she adds three royal legs to her now-magical spider and when she has finished she licks her lips and rejoins us and says, "Butterflies are 🐛Mini-Beasts too."

"And they used to be caterpillars," sniffs Dot.

"Absolutely," says Tulip. "But that's MY fact too."

And she fishes a jellybaby from out of her sock and is just about to pop it in her mouth when Gran says, "I should save that for pudding, dear."

"No thank you," says Tulip, biting off the jellybaby's head.

And I cannot believe she is quite so naughty, and Gran is speechless, so I say, "Actually, Dot, here's a Mini-Beast fact SO good it's got to be worth double points and you can swap it for both of Tulip's facts."

"What is it?" asks Dot.

" METAMORPHOSIS ," I tell her.

Dot looks blank, but Tulip asks, "Is it a kind of beetle, Minnie?"

"No," says Gran, snatching the words right out of my mouth. "But Minnie will tell you if you finish your quiche."

Dot and Tulip amazingly start nibbling, and Gran whispers, "What have you been doing, Minnie?" But I cannot tell her *puzzling a riddle* as I do not want Dot or Tulip to know. So I tell her about MORSE, and how we're getting Australian penfriends, and when Dot and Tulip have gobbled every crumb, I tell Dot that METAMORPHOSIS means changing from a caterpillar into a butterfly.

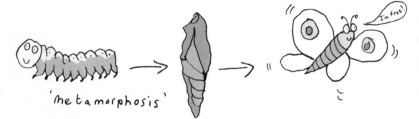

'metamorphosis'

I'm free

I write it down and very carefully Tulip and Dot copy it and, whilst I help take the plates to the kitchen, Gran says, "What did you want to show me, Minnie?"

"It's in my coat," I tell her. And I run to fetch my riddle, only Dot has already beaten me to it!

"Dot!" I squeal. "What are you doing?!"

"Tulip told me to," sniffs Dot, her hands in my pocket. "I told her you had a secret and she wants to see it. Specially as it's got ladybirds on which are Tulip's best Mini-Beast ."

And I am thinking Dot and Tulip are Mini-Beasts , but say, "Next time, Dot, ASK!!"

"OK," says Dot. And so she asks! "Can I do looking at your Mini-Beast secret?"

"NO!" I tell her. "It's MY secret!" And Dot's lip trembles and now I feel bad as she doesn't know it's a birthday riddle, and possible LOVE letter, so best-cousin nicely I say, "Here's another Mini-Beast fact. Being afraid of spiders is called ARACHNOPHOBIA!"

"Oh," sniffs Dot. "Can you write it down for me?"

"And ME," says Tulip. "It's MY fact too. Minnie told it to both of us."

"No she didn't," sniffs Dot. "She told it to ME."

"And ME!" says Tulip, clenching her teeth.

"And ME!" says Dot, clenching her fists. "AND I'll tell Minnie what her secret birthday present is, and you won't Tulip, because you don't know!"

"What secret birthday present?!" I gulp.

"From your mum," sniffs Dot. "Your dad told my dad, and I heard."

"What is it?!" I squeal. But, before she can answer, in pants Uncle Jeff and he has come to pick up Dot and Tulip. I cannot believe it and it is watching-the-clock, totally annoying as he is never on time, and always late and now I want him to be late he's exactly on time! And Dot completely forgets about my present and runs to her dad to show him her picture of her magical spider!

Gran comes out of the kitchen and one minute later Dot's waving goodbye and she cannot speak as Tulip has sneaked her a handful of **SMARTIES**. Dot has stuffed them all in her mouth and is choking on a rainbow.

But at least I have a moment to show Gran my riddle and I hand her my pink-heart envelope and when she has read it she sighs, "How exciting! A **LOVE** letter and a riddle. The best kind of puzzle ever!"

"D'you really think it's a **LOVE** letter?" I ask. "It could just be a riddle."

"Not wrapped up in a pink heart," smiles Gran. "I think you have a secret admirer!"

"And a secret birthday present," I tell her, "that Dot knows about and I don't."

"Oh," says Gran. "Well that's the trouble with secrets. Everybody wants to know them, and nobody wants to tell!"

"And there's nowhere to hide them," I sigh. "If it's not Dot finding my secret riddle, it's Dad finding my secret sweets, or Mum finding my secret puzzlings."

"You need a secret hiding place," laughs Gran.

"I know," I tell her. "But where?"

"How about under your mattress, dear? I always find that works."

"I already do that, but things get *squashed*."

"Hmmmm," thinks Gran. "Maybe you'll find somewhere in your new room."

"Maybe," I sigh. "So what do you think my riddle means?"

"I haven't a clue. But I do think it's something personal, dear, and a riddle that only you should solve."

And Gran is right and Spike is tired and it's time to go home and try!

TUESDAY EVENING

96.00.00

I pop Spike into his buggy and race him home and Mum greets us, covered in paper. "Hi, Minnie ... hi, Spike," she grins. "I've been stripping wallpaper all day."

And the wallpaper she is stripping is in Spike's room because I'm going in there and he's having my dolphin room. And I take a peek to try and see if there's a loose floorboard I could hide things under, or a wobbly brick I could pull out of the wall and stick my secret things behind. But I can't tell, as the floor is covered in torn-off paper and the walls don't have bricks and are still not purple.

Mum says she needs to get changed or she's going to be late for her yoga class and when she has gone Dad says, "Did you solve your LOVE letter, Minnie?"

"We don't KNOW it's a LOVE letter," I sigh. "It's probably just a birthday riddle!"

"So what does it mean?"

"I don't know. AND I don't know what I'm

getting for my birthday from Mum, and Dot does, and I hope it's best-present-ever hair-straightening tongs."

"Are you planning on being a hairdresser?"

"Only on my own hair. I wish I had hair straighteners RIGHT NOW as I'm having my photo taken at school tomorrow and my hair will look like tangled spaghetti and you have to sign this letter giving permission and please can you NOT!"

"I might not if I had a cup of tea," grins Dad.

And I absolutely hate making tea, as I can never get the milk to not whoosh out of the jug, but I smile as sweetly as two sugars and say, "I'll make it if you promise NOT to sign my letter!"

"Promise," smiles Dad. And when I return with a spilling mug he has put the letter to one side and is studying the pictures at the bottom of my riddle. "The clue must be in there," he says.

"I know that!" I tell him. "And if you haven't signed my letter I'm going to bed to try and puzzle out what."

"Only in your dreams," says Dad. "It's 8 o'clock

and girls your age need their beauty sleep."

And I cannot say he is actually wrong because I look nothing at all like a pop star or princess, but I say, "I'm sure tomorrow I'll look exactly the same, even if I close my eyes just this minute."

"Maybe your hair will turn straight overnight!" he laughs.

"Maybe YOU will solve my riddle overnight!" I sigh.

And both of us know this is highly unlikely so I kiss him goodnight and get changed into my too-small Tigger nightie and, with a magnifying glass in one hand and my heart-shaped letter in the other, I get undercover of my dolphin duvet and start some serious puzzling.

And I am trying to decide if it truthfully is a LOVE letter, and if it is, is it really from Kevin. And with the glowing end of my alien pen I look at every

Minnie, here's a riddle
That's my birthday gift to you
Puzzle very carefully
And you will
SPOT THE CLUE!

petal of every rose, and every wing of
every butterfly, and it's very peculiar that
the ladybirds have not been cut from a
magazine, but are drawn by hand and
a bit wobbly. And with the magnifying
glass I stare still closer, and twizzle the riddle
upside down, but it still just looks the same.

And before I've solved anything Mum comes
back from her yoga class and I hide my riddle and
alien pen and she peeps her head around my door
as I pretend I'm totally dreaming of ladybirds. She
goes away to play Scrabble with Dad and when I
hear her say, "You do NOT spell T.R.A.F.F.I.C. like
THAT, Malcolm!" I know I am safe and get back to
my puzzling.

But ten minutes later I'm still puzzled and I give
up and tap on my wall for Wanda Wellingtons. I
decide to teach her more MORSE code, and it's mind-
bogglingly clever because as well as writing MORSE
on to paper, you can also do it by flashing a light on
and off, with a short flash for a dot and a long flash
for a dash. This is specially handy when you don't
have a pen, or it's too dark to see what you've
written.

And as Wanda can't read, I flash my alien pen on and off and give her this secret message:

And hopefully it says TIME FOR BED WANDA WELLINGTONS, but either I've dashed when I should have dotted, or dotted when I should have dash-dashed, or Wanda remembers none of yesterday's lesson, because she has cocked her head to one side awaiting her proper secret signal.

But before I can tap my quilt three times I am suddenly distracted by a dotty idea and I flick my pen back over my riddle and peer at the ladybirds, which do not have any dots or dashes, but DO HAVE SPOTS IN TWO SIZES, medium and small! And the riddle says SPOT THE CLUE so maybe the SPOTS are THE CLUE and the ladybirds' spots are telling me something!

And with MORSE  notes in one hand, and the riddle in the other, Wanda waits patiently whilst I turn the medium-sized spots into MORSE dots and the small spots into dashes. And I spell *R TL* and my brain is fizzing like a sherbet lemon as I think *Really Three Ladybirds* or *Riddle Too Late*. But I have not got the foggiest what it can mean!

So I start again and turn the medium spots into dashes and small spots into dots and so far I have *k E*. And I am suddenly thinking that the next letter is going to be *V* and it's going to spell *KEV*! And my riddle IS a love letter from Kevin Little after all!

And the last ladybird's spots are 🐞 and I go straight to the V, but love-letter-crushingly V is ···—! And now I don't know if I'm happy or sad because, although I didn't want it just to be a LOVE letter, it was kind of nice that it might have been, especially from the dreamiest boy in my class. But I start again and work through the letters and there are only Y and Z to go, and in the next moment I HAVE CRACKED THE CODE! And it doesn't matter that it doesn't say KEV, because dot-and-dash brilliantly it says KEY! And what do KEYS solve? ONLY SECRET CODES, OF COURSE!

Someone knows I'm an undercover-puzzler studying MORSE and I bet it's Gran! She's the best riddler ever and will probably send me a key to a code and secret codes are the best puzzles ever! I can't wait to tell Frankie, and I stuff my things beneath my mattress, in the only secret place I have, and Wanda jumps up and licks my face before curling into a fluffy ball at the bottom of my bed. Totally quietly I whisper, "Minnie to Wanda, over and out," and we both fall fast asleep.

And tonight I dream that my new bedroom is covered in ladybirds that spell

WEDNESDAY MORNING

Dad was wrong and my hair has not turned straight overnight, so I schlurp my Rice Krispies and calculate how many hours till my best party ever. And whilst Mum nibbles her breakfast and tries to work out how I got KEY from three ladybirds, I get out my countdown list and cross out 99 $^3/_4$ and jot 82 $^1/_2$. Then I try to work out if this gives me enough time to "metamorphose" from a curly-haired caterpillar to a smooth-winged butterfly but, before I can, Dad taps his watch and says, "Your bus leaves in six minutes, Minnie, and you're not properly dressed."

"OK," I sigh. "But call me when the postman comes. I'm expecting a key to a secret code!" And I whizz to my room and my cardie has a stain down the front but I don't have time to search for a clean one, and Wanda is chewing my only clean socks so I have to wear my funky caterpillar tights instead. Plus there's not a hair bobble anywhere, and I cross my fingers that someone at school will have one I can borrow. And I fetch today's Party

Clues and there's only two minutes and 35 seconds to catch my bus. I'll have to run even faster than yesterday and Mum shoves a piece of paper in my pocket and fingers crossed it's the key to another puzzling code, but I cannot read it as I'm flying down the stairs and out to the street. The bus is coming and Trevor and Tiff are already there and I have to call out to them to hold the bus and unusually nicely Tiffany pretends she has lost her bus pass and by the skin of my teeth I make it.

"Thanks, Tiff," I puff, as I sit next to Frankie.

Frankie looks at my wind-swept hair and says, "Have you been in a hurricane, Minnie?" And Tiffany sits across the aisle and now I can't tell Frankie about my Ladybird KEY.

"Can I have the window seat?" I whisper to Frankie.

"It's my turn, remember? Or have you lost your brain cells as well as your hair bobble?"

"I need to tell you the answer to my riddle!" I whisper. And two seconds later we are shuffling seats and I huff on the window and doodle,

"What key?" whispers Frankie.

"A CODE key," I tell her. "The three ladybirds spell KEY!"

"How do they do that?"

"In **MORSE**," I whisper. "Their bigger spots are dashes and their small spots are dots!"

"*Foobaroony!*" grins Frankie. "So you're going to get a key to a secret code to crack before your birthday!"

"I think I already have it!" I tell her, and I fish in my pocket for the letter Mum gave me. But it's not a secret key at all, but my consent form for my photograph, signed by Mum!

WEDNESDAY AT SCHOOL

82.00.00

When we get to school I rush into class and I'm about to sneak my Party Clues out when Tiff says, "What are you doing, Minnie?"

"Nothing," I fib, putting the clues back in my bag, and thankfully Mr Impey starts star-jumping and Tiff is distracted and Trevor stops flicking his pencils at my head and miraculously we get one more marble in the marble pot.

"And now we're going to the hall," says Mr Impey, "to have our photos taken for your pen pals."

"Have you got a hair bobble?" I ask Frankie.

"No," says Frankie, her hair loose and smooth and straight. So I try Delilah and Tallulah, and even Brainiac Jenny, but everyone has got their hair loose and completely not tangled so they look photogenically extra special.

I dawdle to the hall wondering how I can escape but, before I can, a thin man with a silly grin is waving me to him and I have to sit on a wobbly stool and grimacingly say CHEESE. And it's a digital camera so there's no chance of my photo going missing in a laboratory or anything and Mr Impey is going to print them on the computer for us, and send them emailingly direct to Australia.

In thirty more minutes I am staring at my photo and I look as if I've been adopted from a peculiar tribe that has no combs or washing machines. And I so hope Mum's present is hair straighteners, but Mr Impey interrupts my thoughts with, "I want you to meet your new penfriends. They've sent an email and a photo, and I've printed them out and paired you with who I think you'll like."

And my penfriend's called Arana and Frankie's is called Ruth and they both look quite nice but I particularly like mine because mind-bogglingly brilliantly Arana likes solving puzzles like me! In her email it says she is ten and lives in a town right on the beach called Darwin and Arana is an aboriginal name which truthfully means MOON. I tell Frankie every detail and how my own name  probably means 'girl with short legs'. And Frankie laughs and I ask, "Do you like Ruth?"

"She's OK," she says. "She likes clothes."

And I take another peek and Ruth is spookily Frankie's real twin with totally sleek black hair. "She looks just like you!" I tell her. "And sounds like you if she likes clothes! She's your secret down-under Australian clone!" And though I can always talk to Frankie I am thinking I would probably not know what to say to perfect Ruth, and I cannot wait to tell Arana about my riddle and maybe she can puzzle the answer!

Tiffany is my computer partner and she always bossily gets to go first and whilst I am waiting I doodle moons in my Exercise Book and scribble Arana on the back of my hand. Usually I'm rubbish at emails and I can never think of what to say, but now I know Arana's a puzzler, I have loads I can tell her about my riddle.

Finally Tiffany signs off and I sign in and tap out my riddle. I explain about the flowers and insects and how the ladybirds are a spotty code that is truthfully **MORSE** which I'm teaching to my dog, Wanda. Then I say about my best-ever party and my

Party Clues and how I cannot believe I'm getting a DJ who's going to be blasting us with the coolest tunes in only ... 78 $^{11}/_{12}$ hours. I amend my countdown list and, irritatingly, it's almost lunchtime. I just have a nanosecond to add **REPLY SOON, Love Minnie x. PS We're having Australian food on Friday. We won't be eating kangaroo will we??!!**

WEDNESDAY AT LUNCH

"What on earth have you been writing?" asks Frankie, as we hide behind the pet shed. "Not even my dad sends an email THAT long!"

"Loads of things," I giggle. "Arana's a specially interesting person because she totally likes doing puzzles like me! How good is that – having a pen-friend who likes puzzles? I'm sure she'll LOVE my birthday riddle, so I told her how it came in a heart-shaped envelope and I thought it was a LOVE letter from Kevin Little, and how the ladybirds spookily spell KEY."

"Oh," says Frankie, staring at my hand and ARANA tattoo.

"And I told her about my mystery invites to my top-secret party as they're full of clues, and puzzlers like Arana LOVE clues. And Mr Impey is so clever to pair me with her as I'd never be able to tell that to Ruth." And I'm just about to add about my DJ when Frankie puts her fingers in her ears.

"What?" I ask.

"There's no need to go on," she groans.

"I didn't know I was," I tell her. "I was just excited because Arana's so nice and…"

"AND you can tell her everything, but you couldn't tell Ruth." And now she is sulking and chewing her hair and I don't know why, so I try a smile, but she still chews. So I suggest handing out my Party Clues and she kind of agrees, but when I race round the playground, dodging Trevor and Tiffany, she lags behind like a sulky snail. And when I hand a clue to Dot, she sighs like she's popped and just deflated and heads back to the pet shed. I warn Dot to keep the clue a secret and am just about to ask what Mum's present is when Tulip Blackberry Tanner arrives. She is holding a woodlouse, which is a heart-racing, scaly Mini-Beast, and whilst Dot squeals with total delight, I decide my mystery present can wait and dash back to Frankie.

"How come Dot got a clue?" she sighs.

"Because Dot's coming to my party of course!"

"She'll just be a nuisance and I bet she's already told Tulip."

"But Dot has to come," I tell her. "Mum says. And she's my cousin."

"You'll be inviting Trevor and Tiffany next!"

"Maybe Tiffany," I suggest. "She's not that bad, and she did hold the bus for me this morning. Plus I'm worried Dot will tell her, even though I've told her it's secret."

"EXACTLY!" grumps Frankie. "Which is why you shouldn't have invited Dot! Dot will tell Tulip and Tulip will tell the whole school and your party will be ruined!"

And now I'm wondering if Frankie is right, and I hand her my Party Clue...

Minnie's TOP-Secret Birthday Party
YOUR 3rd CLUE IS...
Final clue coming soon!

And I'm sure her eyes light up for a flickering moment, but then she remembers she's in a sulk and grumbles, "Does this mean what I think it means?"

"And it's all your idea!" I tell her. And I try to unsulk her by smiling my best-ever friend smile and saying, "I never thought Mum and Dad would agree, but the disco has got everything…"

"Dry ice and a bubble machine!" mopes Frankie. "But what's the point? If Tulip invites the whole school we'll all be packed like sardines and there won't be a spare millimetre for even the tiniest bubble. What are you going to come up with next?"

And she probably thinks I'll say INVITE TREVOR, but I totally won't and I sigh, "The theme, I hope. It's the only thing I haven't planned and I hoped you could help me. I was wondering about a ladybird party and we could all come in red and black, with spotty messages on our backs and we have to find out what they say."

"Sounds great!" groans Frankie. "You know I'm totally rubbish at codes. Though I'm sure interesting ARANA would LOVE it."

And I didn't mean to upset her so I say, "Would you like to come to tea tomorrow?"

"To solve clues?" sulks Frankie. "That'd be fun."

"No," I tell her. "To see my new bedroom and maybe I could show you my party clothes."

"Is that ALL you think I like, Minnie? Just because Ruth likes clothes and you think I look like her ... and sound like her ... does that mean you can't tell me anything else because you couldn't tell Ruth?"

"No!" I sigh. And the bell goes and we head back to class and Frankie goes in with Jenny, not me.

WEDNESDAY AT SCHOOL

This afternoon we study **MORSE** and I decide I'm going to pay extra attention just in case I get sent more ladybirds. Plus it will take my mind off Frankie who won't let me talk to her.

I know the **MORSE** for MINNIE off by heart and Mr Impey is writing

W .__ S... L ._..

on the board, which are our new letters to learn. And like a secret spy I scribble them down, and Mr Impey says we have to pretend we are in the war and write a message so secret our lives depend on it so we have to get it right. And I absolutely do not like war, but I do like Frankie and I decide I will write her something funny to try and cheer her up. And with my strawberry and liquorice scented gel pens I fragrantly doodle

And I make it as totally special as I can, and add butterflies and flowers and a secret sulky snail and when I have finished I sneak it to Frankie. But Frankie ignores it and Tiffany tuts, "Me, me, me, I want to see it!" And I'm worried Tiff's going to get to it first, and even though she's not acting like it, I'm hoping Frankie's still my best friend and will know what I'm thinking. And I cross my fingers and Frankie suddenly pays attention and like an angry bee she darts at the message and hides it from Tiff beneath her desk.

And ten minutes later she's nearly smiling and says, "Wanda Wellingtons ate your socks."

And this means she has cracked my message so I write her another, but this time I do it in real MORSE as I don't want Tiffany getting her hands on my ladybirds! And mind-bogglingly cleverly I write

-- -·-- ·--· ·- ·-· ·· - ·-- --

·· ··· ·· --·

- ·-- --- ·-- · · --·- ···

57

And, as I imagined, Tiffany grabs it and it takes her for ever to puzzle it out, and I think she might actually die of starvation if her life truthfully depended on it. But she finally cracks it and smirks, "Minnie's having a party in two weeks!"

And, twin-like, Frankie knows what I'm up to, but at the end of school Kevin whispers, "Everyone is confused, Minnie. We must have deciphered your clues wrong because we all thought your party was on Saturday."

"It is," I whisper back. "I'm just tricking Tiffany because she's not invited."

"Got you!" nods Kevin, and runs off to spread the word. And when I look up Frankie has gone.

WEDNESDAY AFTER SCHOOL

I catch the bus home, but I have to take Dot and this is annoying as Dot insists on sitting by me, and just at a time when I need to try and be nice to Frankie. But Frankie has sat herself next to a lady with three bags of shopping and she's scrunching up her nose as if something's smelly and I don't actually know what. I'm at my bus stop before I find out and me and Dot wave, and Frankie fans her nose and makes a dash for our empty seats.

I'm pretty sure she's still upset, but it's too late to ask and, what's even more annoying, is that Dot is coming to my place for tea. I race her there and when we get in Mum's in the hall, and I stick my nose round my new-room door and it's still not purple so I whisper, "Did I get any post, Mum?"

"Yes!" giggles Mum, dipping into her overall pocket. And she hands me a turquoise triangular envelope that says *OPEN WEDNESDAY!*

I'm desperate to obey but, like the cling-on she is, Dot comes nosing and I have to stuff it into my pocket. And I'm just thinking I must not leave it hanging around, as Dot might go snooping again, but I can't think of anywhere good to hide it. I cannot reach the top of my wardrobe and none of my drawers have locks on them and there is absolutely nowhere that's secret or Dot-proof.

Five minutes later Dad comes home and Dot sniffs, "Do you know how to make  Mini-Beasts, Uncle Malcolm? I have to make one for school."

"Well I know how to make Minnie into a beast!" he laughs. "Just tease her about her hair."

And I immediately turn into a mad creature and say, "Dad, that's not even funny and it's why I need hair straighteners!" And I head to my bedroom, as Mum calls Dot into the kitchen, and I prise open my turquoise envelope and pull out … a KEY!

And it's a tiny, shiny, SILVER KEY and not a key to a code at all! And I'm madly wondering what it will open, when I unfold a triangle of turquoise tissue, and this is what it says:

We're the rogues of the high waters
Of whom many tales are told
And with parrots on our shoulders
We hunt the seas for GOLD!
WHO ARE WE?

- - - - - - -
1 2 3 4 5 6 7

And I read it again and I'm sure it's *PIRATES* and
I count the letters and they spookily fit and it seems
much too easy and I have no idea what pirates have
got to do with my birthday, UNLESS … the key's
going to unlock a treasure chest and the treasure's
going to be mine! But it's very peculiar that there's
not a code or ladybird anywhere, though at least I
know who's sending the riddles – and it's not GRAN!
It just has to be … MUM! Mum is totally mad on
pirates, especially if they are Johnny Depp!
And, as if she knows I have found her out,
she is calling me, and Dot is her parrot and
calling me too, and two seconds later she
is in my room and trying to peek at MY riddle!

"Are you doing another Mini-Beast secret?" she sniffs.

61

"Possibly," I tell her, "but it's too grown-up for girls who are five."

And her lip trembles as she snivels, "Then can you do coming in the kitchen, Minnie, because Aunty Audrey wants you?"

"All right," I sigh, feeling slightly bad, but I fold the tissue and carefully post it back in its envelope and quickly tuck it under my pillow which is the only place I can think to hide it. I stuff the key beneath my mattress and follow Dot into the kitchen and Dot says she is going to make a Mini-Beast spider.

"Don't tell Dad," says Mum. "Spiders give him the heebie-jeebies and you must never say the 'S' word in front of him!"

I want to tell her about the 'P' word and how I think it's *PIRATES*, but Dot's in the way and Mum is saying, "Pompoms, Minnie! You could make a you-know-what out of woolly pompoms and attach some pipe-cleaners to make its legs."

"I don't do pompoms," sniffs Dot.

"Course you do," says Mum. "Minnie will show you."

And I love making pompoms and I decide I'll make myself a ladybird, so I round up the things we are going to need and sit at the swinging table with Dot. Mum finds some wool and a packet of pipe-cleaners and Dot looks very unimpressed. But when I have cut everything out and made two cardboard rings for me and two cardboard rings for her, we both get busy spinning wool about them, looping it through the hole in the middle. I feel like an 'S' word spinning a web, and sometimes I use red and sometimes black and when the hole has almost vanished, I scissor-snipping carefully cut round the edge and it starts to spring apart. I tie it with wool and tear off the rings and Dot claps because, suddenly, I have a fluffy red spotty pom-pom and at last she cottons on to what she is making.

"I like pompoms!" she sniffs, and Mum is impressed and takes a break from cooking to help me fix the pipe-cleaners for the legs and antennae.

"Can my spider have eleven legs, Aunty Audrey?" asks Dot. "Because mine's a magical queen spider." And Mum attaches six pipe-cleaners to make twelve legs, and snips one in half and Dot is left with an eleven-legged spider.

"Hooray!" sniffs Dot, and Mum says, "Perfect," and Dad secretly whispers, "Perfect is not something I could use to describe tonight's tea. It's something called "HOTPOT, which really means stew."

"You don't like spiders either, do you, Uncle Malcolm?" sniffs Dot.

"Not really," says Dad. "Spiders give me the heebie-jeebies."

"I like spiders," says Dot. "Especially magical queen spiders. They're my best Mini-Beast."

"And I like stew," I tell him, trying to change the subject, "especially with dumplings."

"Girls!" says Dad, giggling at Spike. "Fancy liking spiders and stew!"

And we clear the table and the "HOTPOT looks worryingly lumpy and brown, apart from a chunk of orange carrot that is trying to escape. But it is actually yummily delicious because not only have we got fluffy dumplings, but the lumpy bits are sausages!

And as an extra treat, as soon as we've eaten, Dot has to go home. Mum asks if I can run her back, which is fine by me as I can properly make sure she has definitely gone, but the bad news is it is raining out and no one knows where an umbrella is hiding.

Dot shows Uncle Jeff her spider and says to me, "If I do asking nicely Minnie, can I see your new Mini-Beast ladybirds?"

"What new Mini-Beast ladybirds?" I ask.

"In here," she sniffs. "I borrowed it from under your pillow."

And there, in her hand, is none other than my turquoise envelope!

"Tulip wants a ladybird for her Mini-Beasts collection, but when she tries to catch them they just fly off."

I cannot believe Dot has my riddle and I count down from ten to zero and when I am almost very nearly calm I say, "But there are no ladybirds this time, Dot. And please can I have my envelope back?"

"Yes," sniffs Dot. "But there are ladybirds, Minnie. Lots of them." And she fiddles with the envelope and spookily finds another sheet of tissue! And it looks like another riddle and at the bottom are ten spotty ladybirds!

I try to stay cool and say, "Where did you find it?"

"Behind this bit," sniffs Dot, showing me the now

crumpled sheet of tissue I've already seen. "They were a bit stuck together, Minnie."

"Thanks," I grimace. "And as a reward, I'll draw Tulip a Mini-Beast ladybird."

"Thanks," beams Dot, and she rushes inside and reappears with a red umbrella. "You can borrow this because you're my bestest cousin." And it looks a bit small, but I grab it anyway and Dot gives me back my not-so-secret turquoise secret and says, "Bye, Minnie." And I wave like a bestest cousin should and step back out in the rain.

And I can't look at the ladybirds in the rain so I pop up the umbrella and, though it's small and belongs to a cling-on, it is probably, definitely … the best umbrella on the whole of the planet! And it's not just red, but has black spots, and is a perfect rain-stopping, L A D Y B I R D umbrella!

WEDNESDAY EVENING

Despite the brolly my hair has exploded into a damp mop of curls and when I get in and look in the mirror I look like a cross between a poodle and a sheep. And a very CROSS cross too. "Why can't my hair be straight like Frankie's?" I grumble. "And why can't I have hair straighteners?!"

"Shhh," whispers Mum, "you'll wake Spike. And maybe Frankie would like curly hair ... just like yours."

But I know that she wouldn't, and I don't even know if she likes me, let alone my hair, and I pour myself some juice and escape to the sitting room where I wriggle upside down on the sofa. I'm hoping it will clear my mind and get me into a code-cracking mood instead of just a mood. But my thoughts can't stay focused on PIRATES and ladybirds when it's also thinking about metamorphosing, Dot stealing my things, Dot knowing what my present is (and me forgetting to ask), Tulip inviting the whole school to my party, what theme I should have for my party, and most importantly, how I can make Frankie happy.

And I schlurp my drink, which is not easy when I'm the wrong way up, and now all I can think about is the juice stain on the pink spotty cushion that my head is on and if Mum is going to tell me off. But thankfully nothing spilt on my riddle and, as I cannot seem to solve my problems, I read that instead.

```
We're the rogues of the high waters
    Of whom many tales are told
And with parrots on our shoulders
    We hunt the seas for GOLD!
        WHO ARE WE?

        - - - - - - -
        1 2 3 4 5 6 7
```

```
    Make letters, numbered 1 and 2,
    Walk the plank and disappear!
    We do not need them any more
    We just need these ones here

        - - - - -
        3 4 5 6 7
    You are now on the search for
```

And I'm desperate to get working it out NOW and when Dad comes in I turn myself the right way up and show it to him and whilst he works out *PIRATES* I turn the ladybirds' spots into **MORSE**. But I cannot believe it because it doesn't make sense. It just says ••••• •••—— —•••• ••••— ——••• ••— •••—— —•••• which is not **MORSE** for anything, except ••— = U.

"Perhaps the riddler's changed his spots," laughs Dad, "and made up a new code!"

"That's not fair," I sigh. But I try again, and I do it so slowly Dad's nearly snoring, but the answer's just the same.

"Why not phone Gran?" says Dad.

And this is actually a brainwaving idea, but first I find Mum and say, "If it's you who's sending the riddles, Mum, I think you've made a mistake in the code."

And she does not go red, but stays totally calm and says, "Of course it's not me sending the riddles, Minnie! Why ever did you think that?"

"Because you like pirates," I tell her, "and my last riddle spells *PIRATES*."

"But I don't like spelling pirates," she laughs, "I

69

just like watching them on telly."

"Hmmm," I wonder, "then look me in the eye and say it's not you."

And she bends down and stares for the count of twenty-three and doesn't even blink before saying, "It's not me." So I give up and run to the hall and tap in Gran's number and tell her how the ladybirds are truthfully MORSE in disguise. Gran says, "Fancy that!" and now I'm thinking that maybe the riddler is actually her!

"I think the riddler's made a mistake," I tell her, "because this time the ladybirds' spots are not MORSE, apart from dot, dot, dash which spells U."

"Hmm," says Gran, "maybe the other ladybirds aren't spelling LETTERS. Maybe they're spelling something else!"

"But they can ONLY spell letters. Mr Impey taught us."

"Oh," says Gran. "But has he taught you numbers, dear? MORSE can also spell those."

"Really?" I squeal. And now I'm SURE the riddler is Gran, as only she would know a thing like that.

"You're a genius, Gran! Can you tell me how to do it?"

"I'm afraid not, dear. It was all such a very long time ago that I had to learn things like that. You'll have to ask Mr Impey tomorrow."

"Oh," I sigh, "but it's solving-a-riddle, totally important. Even if it's you who's the riddler, Gran, you could still tell me and give me a clue."

Gran laughs and says, "Of course I'm not the riddler, dear! Now what else did you do today?"

And I'm sure she's just trying to change the subject, but I say, "I got my penfriend and she lives in Darwin and we've got so much in common except she has a garden that parrots live in and I have a balcony with woodlice. She's even a puzzler just like me and her name is Arana which means moon."

"That's nice," says Gran. "I was called Blossom because there was blossom on the cherry trees when I was born though I was nearly called Cherry instead."

"I like Blossom more than Cherry," I tell her.

And Gran agrees and says, "Arana will be fast asleep now, dear. She'll already be in tomorrow."

"Will she?" I ask. "How can anyone be in tomorrow when it's truthfully and actually still today?"

"Because Darwin time is eight hours ahead of ours and right now it will be four in the morning."

"Oh, yes, Mr Impey taught us that." And then I tell her about Frankie, and how I think I've upset her and don't know what to do.

"Invite her to tea," says Gran, "and show her she's special."

"I kind of did," I tell her. "But I don't know if she's coming."

"Then ring her and ask her again. That's what friends are for, dear. Perhaps you've gone on about Arana too much and hurt Frankie's feelings. Is Arana Frankie's penfriend too?"

"No," I tell her. "Frankie's penfriend is called Ruth and she's so much like Frankie she could be her twin, but I'm glad I didn't get her because she's a bit boring and not nearly as nice as Arana."

"And did you tell Frankie this?"

"Yes," I mumble. "Which is why she's upset, I think. But I didn't mean it like that. Frankie's my best-ever, best, best friend and…"

72

"Ring her," says Gran. "Hang straight up on me, dear, and ring her at once. You must tell her you're sorry you hurt her feelings, and that you didn't mean to, and you really want her to come to tea."

And this is why I like Gran, because she always knows just what to do. And I say, "Thanks, Gran."

And Gran says, "You're welcome, dear."

And I phone Frankie, and Frankie says, "Hi," but that's it, and when I ask if she's coming to tea, all she says is, "Maybe."

"I don't want you to look at my party clothes," I tell her. "Or solve clues. I just want you to come as you're my best-ever friend."

"What about puzzling Arana?" says Frankie. "Isn't she your new best friend?"

"No!" I tell her. "Of course she isn't, she's just a nice penfriend, but she isn't special like you."

"But you've got so much in common and we haven't. I'm rubbish at codes and…"

"But Arana couldn't think of fun things like you do, like coming up with a theme for my party. And I know *you* could because you're specially the best at things like that."

"Maybe," says Frankie.

"And I know I've been stupid, and I didn't mean to compare you with Ruth. You can think of loads of things besides clothes. You're a whizz at coming up with ideas."

"But you doodled moons in your Exercise Book and Arana on your hand."

"Not any more," I fib. "I've rubbed the moons out and washed Arana off and got Frankie instead."

"Really?" asks Frankie.

"Really," I say, licking my hand and rubbing at the A and R.

They are just coming off when Frankie says, "I did think a Purple Party might be good."

"That's the best theme ever!" I squeal. "I knew you'd think of something totally brilliant!"

"Everyone has got to wear something purple," she says, "EVEN THE BOYS!" And she seems nearly like her old self and almost as excited as I am.

"Perfect," I tell her. "Because I've already got something purple to wear!"

"What?" giggles Frankie.

"Are you sure you want to know?"

"Course I do, Doodle Noodle!"

"OK. Well I've got a purple skirt, with three layers and it's kind of shiny a bit like silk."

"Fabaroony," says Frankie. "What else?"

"A white top with puffed sleeves and purple flowers embroidered round the neck, and a glittery pair of purple tights with even glitterier silver hearts."

"Ooh," says Frankie, "I can't wait to see it."

"You will," I tell her, "if you come to tea."

"Try and stop me," laughs Frankie. "And did you get more ladybirds?"

"Kind of," I tell her. "But the spots aren't letters and Gran thinks they might be numbers, and I think SHE might be the riddler. And guess what! The KEY is not a key to a code, but a real metal, lock-opening kind! It came with my riddle and is totally tiny and sparklingly silver."

"Fabiozo," says Frankie. "Bring it all to school tomorrow and we'll try and puzzle the MORSE numbers."

"OK," I say. "We can ask Mr Impey and work it out at lunch."

And then Mum shouts, "Is that phone superglued

75

to your ear, Minnie, or can somebody else use it?"

And I whisper to Frankie, "Got to go. I'll see you on the bus tomorrow." And Frankie says bye and I put down the phone and Dad says it's time for bed.

I go to the bathroom and clean my teeth and wash ARANA off the back of my hand and climb into bed and tattoo FRANKIE and rub out every moon I have doodled. Then I stare at the ceiling and think, *IF the ladybirds ARE numbers, what am I supposed to do with them?* They can't be the code to a pirates' gold-filled safe because then why would I need my key? But it's such a plain and boring ceiling that there's nothing to help me puzzle the answer.

And I feel for the key under my mattress and breathe-again-thankfully it's still there and Dot hasn't pinched it and it's actually a good hiding place, even though it makes some things *squashed*. But it's better than my pocket and under my pillow and *squashed* is totally better than stolen. And I grab my Exercise Book and copy the new ladybirds into it so I can solve them with Frankie tomorrow.

When I have finished I think about having a PURPLE party and it's such a good idea I don't know why I didn't think of it myself. And I need to write a Purple Party Clue and I look at my ladybirds and they give me a pencil-fiddling artistic idea. I decide I will decorate my clue in the same sort of way, not with ladybirds, but butterflies. And under Minnie's Top-Secret Party I doodle six, and they are purple with dots and dashes on their wings which cryptically spells PURPLE! And underneath I draw a lettuce-green caterpillar that is waiting to turn into a butterfly!

And it looks totally brilliant and I just need Dad to scan it on the computer in the morning and print me some off. And I look at the caterpillar, which is just like me, and the butterflies, which are beautiful like Frankie, and I count the hours till my Purple-Best-Ever-DJ party. It is 70 and 6 minutes and I note this on my countdown list and wonder if it will give me enough beauty sleep to "metamorphose".

If there's the teeniest chance I decide I'll take it because, if my party's going to be the best ever, then I need to look my best ever and I wonder if anyone in my class has hair straighteners I could borrow. I decide I'll ask the girls tomorrow, and stuff my riddles and pens and Exercise Book under my mattress and tap on my wall for Wanda Wellingtons. And there's no time to waste on flashing MORSE, so I tap my duvet three times and Wanda jumps up and licks my face and curls into a fluffy ball.

And tonight I dream I am saving Dad from a spider in a cherry tree and I'm scaring it with a caterpillar and the caterpillar is me.

THURSDAY MORNING

After yesterday's fiasco with my whirlwind hair, and my quest to try and metamorphose, I decide to try extra hard to look better. I experiment with plaits but I just look like Tiff, and bunches make me look like a white spaniel, so I give up and stick in a hair slide and I'm just getting in a bad mood when the postman has a card for me and it's all the way from France!

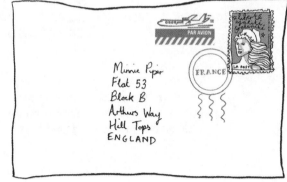

It's probably, definitely from Aunty Valerie, Dot's mum, and Dad has to sign to say that we've got it. And, as if this is not exciting enough, there's also a round purple envelope which says

OPEN THURSDAY!

And inside is a new riddle!

What you seek won't come to you,
In your mission you may fail
If you cannot follow all the clues
From the pirate ship you sail.
But it's not upon high waters
You must travel in your quest,
But through the streets of Hill Tops
To do what you do best.
All clues are there for those who see,
They just lie in disguise
And when you have unpuzzled them
They'll be right before your eyes!
So Minnie, if you're ready,
The first I'll now unfold
YOU SHOULD SEEK OUT THE SHOP WINDOW
WHERE THE SPICES ARE NOT COLD!

PS
You must take someone with you
On your treasure laden quest,
And may I suggest your father
Is quite probably the best!

"Dad!" I squeal. "These riddles are from you!"

"I don't think so," laughs Dad. "But these are!"
And he hands me my Purple Party Clues.

"But it's highly suspicious that it recommends
taking YOU with me."

"And even MORE suspicious as to where you have to go," laughs Dad. "What does YOU SHOULD SEEK OUT THE SHOP WINDOW WHERE THE SPICES ARE NOT COLD mean?"

"I don't know," I tell him. "But I bet YOU do and you're just trying to pretend that you don't!"

And he looks at the riddle and says, "I could never make up a poem like that." And annoyingly this is totally true, and it's even more annoying that my new riddle says, 'So Minnie, if you're ready,' because I haven't actually solved yesterday's riddle yet and I am not ready at all. But I have to run if I'm going to catch the bus and I race as fast as my short legs can, and surprisingly they are speedily nippy and I get there with nearly a minute to spare.

But now I have to say nice things to Tiff, who asks, "Am I coming to your party, Minnie?"

And I try not to gulp and I feel so bad that this time my tongue is truly tangled and feels too big for my mouth. "Maybe," I mumble, crossing my fingers. "I'm not sure what I'm doing yet."

"Oh," says Tiff. And breathe-again thankfully the bus arrives and I've never been so pleased to see Frankie!

81

"Hi," says Frankie, as I sit beside her. She's smiley and friendly but there's something teensily peculiar about her and she seems a bit twitchy and is nibbling her nails. Tiffany sits across the aisle and there is only a grubby half a metre between us and this is not enough to share secrets without being found out. So instead of telling Frankie about my new riddle I just say, "Hi," back.

"Are you trying to look nice for Daniel Jackman?" asks Tiff, looking at my hair slide.

"NO!" I tell her. "I am just making up for yesterday."

"Then why did you write DJ on the window?"

"Because!" I tell her. And then I totally ignore her and ten seconds later she gives up and goes to sit by Tulip.

"Phew," sighs Frankie, sucking her hair. "Tiff's such a pain."

"And she wants to know if she's coming to my party."

"What a cheek! You never said yes, did you, Minnie?"

"Maybe," I mumble.

"Maybe you said yes?! Has your brain got

frazzled with all these riddles?"

"I only said maybe. Maybe she could come. I couldn't think of what else to say."

"How about NO?" sighs Frankie. "It's very easy. Repeat after me, N...O spells NO!

"No," I sigh. "But speaking of riddles, I got a new one this morning." And I'm about to show her when we arrive at school, and I stick the purple envelope into her hand. She's just going to look when Tiffany sneaks up and says, "Tulip says your party is THIS SATURDAY, Minnie. Not in two weeks! And I know it's a Purple Party and I bet that's a purple invite." And she glares at the purple envelope in Frankie's hand, and Frankie goes scarlet and nervously shoves it into her pocket.

"It's just a prototype," I tell her, "which means Frankie is testing it and if she thinks it's a good idea then *maybe* it will be on Saturday and *maybe* it will be a purple party and…"

"And maybe I can come?" says Tiff.

"Maybe," I sigh. "Maybe."

THURSDAY AT SCHOOL

It takes 151 star jumps for Class Chickenpox to settle, but as soon as we have I say, "Do you know **MORSE** numbers, Mr Impey?"

Mr Impey grins and says, "Actually I do, Minnie. We were going to learn them next week, but maybe, as you've mentioned it, we could look at them now."

"Great!" groans Trevor. "Trust you, Piper."

But now I'll be able to test Gran's theory, and I get out my Exercise Book and let Frankie see the moons have gone, and open it on to the ladybird page. Mr Impey scribbles on the board and says, "Copy this down and we can have some fun."

"Are you gonna give us chocolate biscuits then?" asks Trevor.

"No," says Mr Impey, "we're going to do **Sudoku** and it's all about filling a grid with numbers, and you need each number from one to nine in every row, across and down. Only to make it more fun, we'll do it in **MORSE**."

This is doubly exciting as Gran has just started teaching me **Sudoku** and it's just a question of sorting numbers into a special order. But Frankie is completely unaware of anything numerical because she is reading my purple letter! And she is so excited she starts waving it in the air and Mr Impey sees and says, "I think I should have that, Frankie," and takes it to lock it in his desk drawer!

"But Mr Impey…" I blurt, "it's a very important…" But I cannot say it's a very important **Secret Riddle** because then everyone will know and it won't be secret. So I add, "…document. It's a totally, can't-possibly-lose-it document and I have to have it back."

"At the end of school," says Mr Impey.

And Tiffany shouts, "I know what Minnie's document is. It's a prototype for her Purple Party and Frankie was testing it."

And everyone knows that Tiff's not invited and they nervously look at me and seem to be saying, 'It wasn't me who told her', only they aren't actually using their voices, more their faces and eyes.

"Wot's a prototype?" heckles Trevor.

"This is," smiles Mr Impey, pointing at the board.

85

Minnie Piper

"This is probably the first ever **Sudoku** puzzle that you have to answer in **MORSE**. And being a prototype means it's a kind of test for the real thing to see if it might work."

"Just like Piper's brain," grunts Trevor.

And he turns round and flares his nostrils, and I look him straight in the eye and say, "If you open those nostrils any wider, Trevor, your brain will probably slip out."

And the class laughs and Trevor snorts (because he's tightened his nose), and Mr Impey coughs and says, "Let's get back to our task in hand." And he points to a list of **MORSE** numbers and a grid of nine rows of nine boxes, and he has filled most of them but there are two empty boxes on each line that we have calculatingly got to fill.

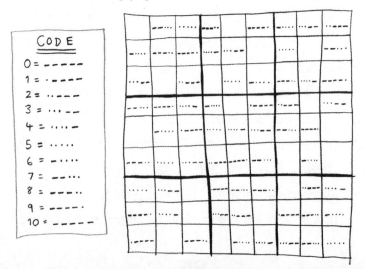

This is perfectly my kind of work, and I'm almost distracted from losing my riddle, because I'm just so keen to get started. I really want to be the first to complete it and I look at Jenny to make sure I get to start before her, but hair-twirlingly frustratingly she has already started! Whilst I have been listening and irritating Trevor, Brainiac Jenny has copied everything down and has very nearly filled three out of eighteen empty boxes. This is don't-want-to-be-last annoying and I start puzzling and converting MORSE numbers and scribbling them down in my own boxes. But I have doodled my grid so fast that some of the boxes are chocolate-cake fat and others celery-thin. And Frankie doesn't want to do it and twitchily whispers, "I told you Dot would tell Tulip about your party!"

"I know," I sigh, "but right now I'm especially keen to think of Sudoku instead."

"Please yourself," jitters Frankie. "But don't blame me if Dot and Tiffany spoil it."

I decide to ignore her as it will take ages to unsulk her and I haven't got time when I've a brainiac to beat. And after fifteen minutes I have actually got sixteen of the missing numbers and I only have two to try and work out. And I think I almost have number seventeen, when Brainiac Jenny is waving her hand and is *Sudoku*ly complete. I cross my fingers in the hope she's gone wrong, but this just makes it harder for me to write my last two numbers. So I give up and Mr Impey says, "Well done, Jenny. Completely correct."

But I know she's also completely a swot and instead of getting too bothered I apply MORSE numbers to the ladybirds in my Exercise Book. And Gran, as always, is totally right because the ladybirds are truthfully numbers, all except the U!

"I've done it!" I whisper to Frankie. And I look at my answer:

Frankie sighs, "Done what? Invited Trevor to your party as well?"

"No," I grin. "I've turned the ladybirds into numbers!"

"Oh," says Frankie. And I can't help but notice she has nearly nibbled her nails away as she says, "But what does 5 3 6 4 7 U 3 6 mean?"

"I haven't a clue," I tell her, "but I can't wait for lunch to try it on my riddle."

And she doesn't say NOR ME, but looks embarrassingly peculiar and fiddles with her hair instead.

THURSDAY AT LUNCH

At lunchtime me and Frankie do not go behind the pet shed as I need to hand out my Party Clues. But Frankie's still acting suspiciously oddly and stays two paces behind like my shadow, looking round the playground as if she's expecting a horrid surprise. This is extra peculiar because it is the final clue to my best ever party and it is her who gave me the purple idea but she is not at all excited. I'm also asking if anyone's got hair straighteners I could borrow for my party, but no one has, which is nearly as irritating as Dot running over and shouting, "Can I have a clue?"

"Shh," I tell her, and I'm almost tempted not to give her one because she told Tulip about my party and Tulip has told Tiffany. But I also don't want to make a fuss and attract more attention so I sneak her the clue and tell her to put it straight in her pocket.

"OK," she sniffs, but she looks at it first and says, "Are there going to be butterflies at your party, Minnie?"

90

"No," I whisper, as Tiff hovers in the distance. "It's MORSE code and it means you have to wear something purple."

"Oh," sniffs Dot. "But I don't do purple, I only do pink."

"Pink's fine," I tell her, as Tiff approaches, and I'm just about to ask her what Mum's present is when Tiff's scarily close and I suddenly panic.

"Have you drawn Tulip's ladybird picture?" asks Dot.

To Tulip
from
Minnie X

Thankfully I have and I fetch it from my bag and Dot beams and says, "Thanks, Minnie!"

And I say, "Go and give it to Tulip right away."

"OK," sniffs Dot, and she disappears and Tiff follows her and sees my picture and not the clue!

Frankie sighs, and says, "So didn't you like my idea that EVERYONE has got to wear purple then?"

"Course I did," I grin, "but I didn't want to make a fuss. Tiff was watching me and I just wanted to get rid of Dot as quickly as possible."

"So now what?"

"Solve my riddle?"

"Fine!" sighs Frankie. "Then you won't need ME. I told you yesterday I'm rubbish at riddles."

"But I thought you said that you wanted to help…"

Frankie slouches off in another sulk and I'm just about to go after her when Tulip runs up to say thanks for her picture and a peculiar thought comes into my head. And it's just as puzzling as all of my riddles, and I'm thinking back to the bus this morning and what I think is HOW COULD TULIP KNOW I WAS HAVING A PURPLE PARTY? I have only just told Dot, yet Tulip already knew on the bus … and Tulip gets on before me just like … FRANKIE!

And it can only be Frankie who could have told Tulip because absolutely no one else knew! And I cannot believe that Frankie would do this, or that I didn't think of it before. But my mind's been so full of pirates and ladybirds. And why would I suspect my best friend?

So that's why she's been acting oddly all morning! I scan the playground to try and find her and she's hiding behind Delilah and Tallulah. I'm so mad, I leave her there and head straight to the pet shed to hide myself. And when I'm totally out of sight I shut out my thoughts and wipe my tears and concentrate on one thing…

We're the rogues of the high waters
Of whom many tales are told
And with parrots on our shoulders
We hunt the seas for GOLD!
WHO ARE WE?

- - - - - - -
1 2 3 4 5 6 7

Make letters, numbered 1 and 2,
Walk the plank and disappear!
We do not need them anymore
We just need these ones here

- - - - -
3 4 5 6 7
You are now on the search for

And peculiarly I know just what to do! All the letters in *PIRATES* are numbered 1 – 7 and then 1 and 2 walk the plank and I'm left with RATES numbered 3 – 7.

And I scribble down

RATES
3 4 5 6 7

So 3 = R, 4 = A.
5 = T
6 = E, and 7 = S!

And the Ladybird code says 5 3 6 4 7 U 3 6. And I replace the numbers with their matching letters and turn 5 into T and 3 into R and 6 into E and 4 into A, and…

...the riddle says:

You are now on the search for

TREASURE

I just need to get my new riddle off Mr Impey and hopefully I can find it!

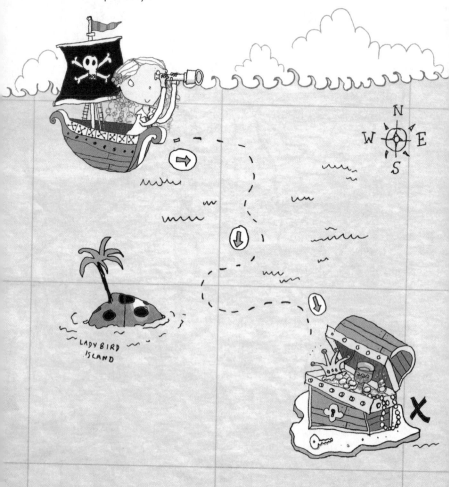

LADYBIRD ISLAND

THURSDAY AFTERNOON

I do not speak to Frankie and she does not speak to me and Mr Impey teaches us about marsupials which are truthfully creatures with built-in pockets and I wish I had one as it would be a good place to hide my secrets. Examples of marsupials are kangaroos and bandicoots and wallabies and possums and I am thinking Australia has specially good names for animals and all we have is cow and cat and worm and slug.

Mr Impey hands out squares of card and we have to paint marsupials on them and discover biological facts and neatly write them across the bottom. I choose a koala bear and Frankie chooses a kangaroo and Tiffany irritatingly copies me and chooses a koala too. But I will not let her copy my discoverings and I put my arm around the card as I scribble *Koalas only eat eucalyptus leaves, which are not nutritiously extra brilliant so they have to mainly take a rest and sit in trees all day. But they* can probably breathe nostrilly well because eucalyptus does that.

And then Dot comes in with a message for Mr Impey and takes a peep at my picture and says, "You should do making it a magical queen koala Minnie, and give it eleven legs."

Tiffany laughs and calls Dot a nincompoop, and Dot looks worried and says, "What's a nin-kong-poop, Minnie?"

And her bottom lip trembles and I'm so mad with Tiffany for being a sneaky copycat, that I tell her, "It's actually a very clever person, Dot, and you have just given me a good idea!" And I take my pencil and doodle seven more legs.

And Tiffany takes her paintbrush and paints her koala seven more legs too! Dot looks happy and goes back to tell Tulip and when she has gone I take out my rubber and totally erase every extra limb.

Tiff says, "Why are you doing that, Minnie?"

"Nincompoop," I tell her. "What koala has got eleven legs!"

And Tiffany stares at her ruined picture and Mr Impey says we can do silent reading for the last ten minutes as he has to work on something for Mrs Elliot.

But I would rather do silent writing instead and, as I need to tackle Frankie, I take a deep breath and scribble, "I KNOW YOU TOLD TULIP ABOUT MY PURPLE PARTY!!!!"

Frankie blushes and swallows hard and fiddles with her hair and scribbles back, "Of course I didn't. Dot did."

"BUT DOT DIDN'T KNOW IT WAS PURPLE!! NOBODY KNEW TILL LUNCHTIME. EXCEPT YOU OF COURSE, WHO JUST HAPPENED TO BE ON THE BUS WITH TULIP BEFORE I GOT ON!"

"But…"

"But what?"

"But … I'm sorry Minnie."

"So it WAS you?!"

Frankie nods and whispers, "But if I hadn't told her, Dot would have."

"But you're my best friend and Dot's a cling-on."

"I know," sighs Frankie, "and I'm sorry, Minnie. Fabaroonily, horribly sorry. But I didn't tell Tulip this morning, I told her last night, just after you got off the bus, when I was still upset that you were comparing me to Ruth, and you said you wouldn't want Ruth as a friend."

"But why would that make you snitch to Tulip?"

"Because I was REALLY upset. I've been secretly planning your party for ages and there are things you don't know and I've tried to think of everything to make it perfect and then you invite Dot who'll make it not perfect. And I only wanted to make my best friend's birthday special, but now I'm not your best friend. Arana is."

"That's not true," I tell her. And I wave my hand with **FRANKIE** doodled on it and say, "I'll even swap you Arana for Ruth. We just need to tell Mr Impey."

"It's OK," says Frankie. "You'd hate Ruth. She's such a show-off."

"Why don't we both have Arana then?! She could be your pen pal too, and we could both share our news. I'm sure Mr Impey wouldn't mind."

"Really?" mumbles Frankie. "You don't mind sharing?"

"Of course I don't! But on one condition?"

"What?" says Frankie.

"You have to help me plan my Purple Party! I can't do it without you."

"OK," she smiles. "Thanks, Minnie. Does that mean I'm still coming to tea?"

"You'd better be," I grin. And the bell goes for the end of school, and  the end of our argument, and Mr Impey gives me back my riddle and Dot is waiting and we run for the bus. Tiffany pulls a face at me all the way home and I tell her she'll probably, definitely stay like it and Dot looks worried as Tulip is teaching her lots of faces and I have to whisper, "Not really, Dot," as we climb the stairs to her flat.

Uncle Jeff invites us in, but Frankie and me say, "We have lots and lots of things to do and we cannot spare a minute."

THURSDAY AFTER SCHOOL

Mum is covered in white spots of paint. "It's an allergic rash to decorating," she laughs. "I've painted the ceiling in your new room."

"Thanks!" I smile, but when I peek in I'm a bit disappointed it's just so boringly white. So me and Frankie go to my old room and jump on my raft-bed and get out my _OPEN THURSDAY!_ riddle.

What you seek won't come to you,
In your mission you may fail
If you cannot follow all the clues
From the pirate ship you sail.
But it's not upon high waters
You must travel in your quest,
But through the streets of Hill Tops
To do what you do best.
All clues are there for those who see,
They just lie in disguise
And when you have unpuzzled them
They'll be right before your eyes!
So Minnie, if you're ready,
The first I'll now unfold
YOU SHOULD SEEK OUT THE SHOP WINDOW
WHERE THE SPICES ARE NOT COLD!

PS
You must take someone with you
On your treasure laden quest,
And may I suggest your father
Is quite probably the best!

I explain to Frankie about the treasure and we guess we are going on a treasure trail, but we don't know where.

"If the spices aren't cold..." I mumble.

"Then they're hot!" laughs Frankie. "What we need are hot spices!"

"Chilli!" I exclaim, "That's HOT." And I am just about to investigate the kitchen when Frankie points out that the riddle says

You must travel in your quest,
But through the streets of Hill Tops
To do what you do best.

And so it is probably not meaning Mum's kitchen ... but, "I know!" I squeal.

And Dad pops his head round my door and says, "What d'you know, Minnie Minx?"

"The answer to the riddle, I think. And I'm pretty, sure we have to go to Jasen's shop!"

"Are we having curry for tea?" asks Dad.

"No," I tell him, "at least I don't think so. But the riddle says, YOU SHOULD SEEK OUT THE SHOP WINDOW WHERE THE SPICES ARE NOT COLD!"

"And Jasen's dad runs an Indian deli!" laughs Dad.

"And we need to go and find his shop window!" shrieks Frankie.

"And don't forget the PS – about taking me too!"

"All right," I sigh.

And Mum shouts from the kitchen, "If you're going out you can take Spike too. And whilst you're there, will you buy some poppadums and mango pickle because I think I will make curry after all."

And so hot-on-the-trail we set off, with Spike in his buggy, and when we get to Jasen's dad's shop we peek through the window and Mr Chawder waves. We traipse in and tell him we're specially keen on hot spices and he points us to the back of the shop to rummage through the packets of chilli ... where we find absolutely nothing at all!

"I don't think we should be in here," I say. "We're supposed to be seeking a window."

So we all go outside and scour the window, and it's a display of exotic fruits and vegetables that have strange names like ladies' fingers and then Frankie points to a section of the window with a group of postcards advertising HOOVER FREE TO GOOD HOME and WINDOW CLEANER AVAILABLE. And then I notice something else! And it's not at all like the other cards, and it doesn't have words – just spotty ladybirds!

And I can read it immediately because they're all the letters in my name, and the card says MINNIE!

"I've found it!" I squeal. And me and Frankie and Dad and Spike all pile back in the shop.

Mr Chawder says, "This is the most peculiar thing I have ever displayed." And I'm just about to explain about the treasure trail, when a customer comes in and

Mr Chawder gives me the card and on the back it says:

> Clue number 2 is in the shop,
> But you do not need to buy.
> It lies within the saddest veg
> That always makes me cry.

"Onions!" I squeal.

And Mr Chawder says, "Right behind you."

And it's an eye-watering job, but I have to do it, and there, in the onion skins at the bottom ... I find a silver-star envelope and together we read

OPEN FRIDAY!

"Fobaroony!" laughs Frankie.

"But I have to wait till tomorrow!" I protest.

"Don't worry," says Dad. "You've got a nice curry to look forward to. And that reminds me, we'd better not forget the poppadums and pickle." And Mr Chawder gives Dad all he needs, plus a bag of Indian sweets for free for making his dull day spicily exciting!

THURSDAY EVENING

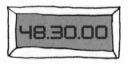

Mum has cooked us an Indian banquet and we have spicy pakoras and yoghurty dip and chicken biryani and Dad puts the poppadums and pickle on the table and when we have finished we all have Mr Chawder's sweets, except for Spike and Wanda.

And then me and Frankie rush to my room and I'm about to show her my party clothes, when I notice ... SPIKE'S COT IS WEDGED AGAINST THE WARDROBE!

"It's only for a few nights," says Mum, when I go to the kitchen to grumble. "I want him to get used to his new room."

And he has to go to bed in fifteen minutes and I only have 900 seconds to drag his cot away to show Frankie my skirt and top.

"Fabaroony!" says Frankie, as I put them on the bed. "You're going to be the belle of the ball."

"Thanks," I smile. "Have you got your dress yet?"

"I might have!" grins Frankie. "But I'm not telling

you till we've planned your Purple Party!"

"OK," I smile. And, as we're now down to 20 seconds, we go to the sitting-room and I fetch some paper and Frankie gets out her purple pen.

We sit at the table and Frankie says, "Have you planned ANYTHING yet?"

"Only that I want it to be the best party ever with the best DJ ever and the best friends ever and that the best purple party needs purple just-about-everything-there-is."

"Like purple balloons!" giggles Frankie. And she lends me her pen and I scribble it down and start a list and Frankie shouts…

"Purple streamers! …And purple confetti… And purple love-hearts…"

And she is thinking so purply, peculiarly quickly that I can barely scribble fast enough!

"Purple icing on a purple cake with eleven purple candles!" she laughs.

And she goes on and on and when we've done everything purple in the universe she thinks about food and every type of crisp and cake and sandwich filling and flavour of pizza and fizzy drinks and how we should arrange the tables and chairs and where we want to sit, and the tunes we need to request from the DJ, and it's the longest list I have ever written!

"Thanks," I giggle, when we cannot think of another thing. "I'm not going to have the best party ever in Arthurs Way, but the best party ever on the planet!"

"I know," laughs Frankie. "It's going to be so fabaroony I needed a fabaroony dress!" And she starts to describe it, but it's so complicated I get her to draw it and she says it has sequins so I fetch her some glitter. And her doodle looks like a sparkling purple hammer, but it's bound to turn her into a purple princess. Then, like Cinderella, she has to go because Fabio has come to collect her. "Bye," she calls, as she skips out the door. "See you on the bus tomorrow. And don't forget to bring your silver-star riddle."

"I won't," I promise. And I give Mum the extra-long list, and she doesn't even blink or grumble.

"I'll see what I can do," she smiles.

It's time for bed and I go to the bathroom to clean my teeth and look in the mirror and I have purple glitter on my right cheek and it must have come from

Frankie's picture. It looks sparklingly nice and I think maybe I should try it for my Purple Party. And I am so happy that Frankie has thought of so many things to make my party special and I wonder what the things are that I don't even know about. I barely even mind that I'm sharing with Spike, and I count the hours until my birthday, and jot 46 on my countdown list with Frankie's purple pen. She left it behind and … and I remember back to our MORSE words and how I chose RIDDLE and KEVIN L because they were written in purple and… So it was Frankie and not Kevin! Frankie must have hidden her pen!

And this reminds me to hide my star riddle under my mattress and then I climb into bed and knock on my wall for Wanda Wellingtons. Ten seconds later we are both snoring and tonight I dream I'm in my new bedroom and the floor is made from poppadums and my bed is a red-hot chilli.

FRIDAY MORNING

As soon as I wake up, I reach under my mattress for my silver-star clue. It's a bit wrinkly where I've been lying on it, but I can still read it and this is what it says:

My first is in PIRATE, but not in PARROT
My 2nd in MARROW, but not in CARROT
My 3rd is green and small and round
And lots of them are often found
Upon your plate beside a kipper
And two of them are in my slipper!
My 4th comes right before an F
(before an A in HEAR and DEAF!)
My last is WHY and is not WHO
My whole is clever - just like YOU!

At the end of the day, before the bell
This is what you need to tell...
Ask what it might signify
It brought us peace, but find out why.
Then seek the statue where it's said,
There lies a gallant soldier, dead.
What's his name?

There are two riddles and two Ladybird codes which makes it doubly mind-bogglingly exciting and I can't wait to get puzzling. But right now I've a breakfast to gulp and a uniform to put on and I've not got a second to spare for riddles if I'm going to catch my bus. Ten minutes later I am grabbing my bag (which does not contain a packed lunch because we are going to be eating Australian tucker), and Frankie has saved me the window seat and I secretly show her my new riddle.

"What does that mean, Poodle Noodle?!"

"I don't know," I tell her. "Perhaps we can work it out at lunch."

"We'd better," says Frankie, "because we need to tell something before the end of school bell. But how do we know who we have to tell? Perhaps it says in Ladybird code?"

"Maybe, but I've a sneaky suspicion it's numbers again. I recognize ·---- which is number 1."

"You are numerically much too clever," says Frankie. And I take out my Exercise Book and sneak a peek at yesterday's notes and Frankie is right AND I am right and the first ladybirds are MORSE numbers! And one by one I doodle the answer on to the window, and it says 1481945. Tiffany leans over us and says, "Are you doing **Sudoku**, Minnie?"

"No," I tell her. "And if I was it would be totally wrong as you can only have one of each number in every line and there are two 1's and two 4's!"

"No need to shout," says Tiff. "I was only trying to be nice."

"More like creeping," whispers Frankie, when we get off the bus. "She's after an invite to your Purple Party."

"I know," I sigh. And we run into school before she can catch us and Mr Impey is in his Friday-black tracksuit, and spinning about like a whirligig beetle. We take 69 star jumps to settle and earn a marble and when we are quiet he announces, "Good news, Chickenpoxers. You have replies from your Australian penfriends."

"I'll ask him if we can both share Arana," I whisper to Frankie.

"Don't worry," says Frankie. "I think I'll get on better with Ruth, and it wouldn't be nice to abandon her."

"Are you sure?" I ask.

"Sure," says Frankie. And we have to team up with our computer partners and Tiffany always wants to go first, but this morning she's had a brain transplant and says, "I'll go last if you like, Minnie."

And I know she is probably, definitely creeping, but I say, "Thanks, Tiff," and race to a computer and log on and search my mail. And there it is … all the way from Australia!

> **From: Arana**
> **To: Minnie**
>
> Dear Minnie, How cool is that getting ladybird clues! I've been secretly puzzling your riddle and the code under my desk whilst we were sposed to be having spelling. But who wants to know how to spell PUTRID when it's just about food going mouldy. And talking of food, hope you enjoy your Aussie tucker. Sometimes we do eat kangaroo, but it's mainly _._. .... _ _ _ _ _ _ _._ and a few ... _. ._ _ _. … chucked on the barbie!
> Happy munching and happy puzzling,
> Your pen-buddie, Arana xxx

And I cannot believe it but Arana has sent me **MORSE** code!

I tell Frankie and Frankie laughs and says it's a good job Arana is NOT her penfriend because her head is swimming with **MORSE** already, what with Mr

Impey's lessons and my Ladybird code. "Who wants MORSE from your penfriend too?!"

"I do!" I tell her, and I email Arana my riddle about PARROTS and CARROTS and the gallant soldier and the new Ladybird code in real MORSE. And at last I sign off and, whilst Tiff signs on, and Frankie reads her email from Ruth, I start cracking Arana's code. And it's very peculiar because it spells CHOOK and SNAGS and I have no idea what this means and it is totally worrying that I have to eat it!

And for the rest of the morning we finish our marsupial pictures and just before lunch I whisper to Frankie, "Do you think we'll have to eat chook and snags?"

"I hope not," worries Frankie. "What are they?"

"I'm not sure. It's what Arana told me in MORSE code. I hope it isn't Aussie for snakes!"

"I'd rather starve," shivers Frankie.

"Me too," I giggle. And when Mr Impey says, "Who's hungry then?" me and Frankie do not wave our hands. But everyone else is waving theirs because they do not know about chook and snags. And Mr Impey seems to read my mind and, whilst I am thinking of baked koala, he writes CHOOK and SNAGS and TUCKER on the board! Talk about putting people off! And then he says, "Who can tell me what these are?"

Everyone looks at Brainiac Jenny, but it's Tallulah who answers, and instantly my stomach stops heaving because chook is only Aussie for CHICKEN! And SAUSAGES are snags! How good is that? And they are ready and waiting in the dining hall, and now I can't wait to get stuck in and it smells delicious and there's not a kangaroo or koala in sight and it is probably, definitely my best lunch ever!

FRIDAY LUNCHTIME

As soon as we've finished munching, me and Frankie run to the pet shed because we urgently need to solve my riddle.

My first is in PIRATE, but not in PARROT
My 2nd in MARROW, but not in CARROT
My 3rd is green and small and round
And lots of them are often found
Upon your plate beside a kipper
And two of them are in my slipper!
My 4th comes right before an F
(before an A in HEAR and DEAF!)
My last is WHY and is not WHO
My whole is clever - just like YOU!

At the end of the day, before the bell
This is what you need to tell...
Ask what it might signify
It brought us peace, but find out why.
Then seek the statue where it's said,
There lies a gallant soldier, dead.
What's his name?

PARROT
PIRATE

I get out my Exercise Book and think, if the 1st letter's in PIRATE and not PARROT, then it cannot be P or A or R or T, which only leaves I or E. So I jot these down and do exactly the same with MARROW and CARROT. "M or W," giggles Frankie.

"Correct!" I tell her, moving on to letter number 3, which is green and round and there are two in slipper and we both shout out "P!" The 4th letter has got to be E as it comes before F in the alphabet and before A in HEAR and DEAF. And now we just need the very last one and the clue is right there – my last is Y! And we look at what we've got and we have

I/E   M/W   PEY

"Impey!" I giggle. "The answer's IMPEY, Mr Impey, and HE's clever just like ME!"

"Fobaroonly!" laughs Frankie. "Perhaps it's him who's sending the riddles!"

"Could be!" I grin. "He does know all the MORSE numbers which even Gran didn't know."

"And he likes codes," says Frankie. "But does he know it's your birthday, Minnie?"

"Maybe," I say. "Tiff talked about it in class, remember?"

"But that was AFTER your first riddle."

"That's true. I'll just have to ask him."

"Ask him at the end of the day because we have to tell him about the numbers remember. 1481945."

"Oh, yes!"

And we puzzle the last ladybird code...

...and it says I E, and we are just trying to work out what this can mean, and how 1481945 brought us peace, when we are brought a cling-on cousin instead. "Hi, Dot," I sigh, hiding the riddle in my pencil case.

"Hi, Minnie. Can I do bringing Tulip to your Purple Party? She really wants to come."

Frankie glares at me and shakes her head, and I am just about to shake in agreement when I change my mind and say, "OK, but on one condition. You have to tell me what my present from Mum is!"

"OK," sniffs Dot. "She's doing painting..."

"But I already know she's doing that. I planned it with her and chose the paint and I've already seen my painted white ceiling."

"And she's painting a—"

"A wall too, Dot. I DO KNOW!"

"Not just a wall, a—"

"Another wall, and another two walls after that! You cheated, Dot."

"Didn't," she sniffs. "And I'm still bringing Tulip because you just said."

And, before I can turn her into a slug, she rushes away to tell Tulip she can come to my party ... my best-ever Purple Party. And Frankie sighs at what I have done, and says, "You're mad, Minnie Piper!"

"I know," I groan, and the bell goes and we march back to class.

FRIDAY AFTERNOON

We have to help Mr Impey stick our marsupial pictures up and he arranges them so that they look ever so slightly like a map of Australia if you close one eye and squint with the other. Tiffany is upset that her koala bear has eleven legs and she has tried to paint over them with green leaves, but it has just made a mess. She's been very quiet all afternoon and Delilah tells me my secret is out and Tiffany knows that everyone in the class is going to my party and I'm having a DJ and dry ice. And now I feel bad and Tiff looks so sad that I march right up to her and say, "Of course you can come to my party, Tiffany. I must have mislaid your invitation, but I definitely want you to come."

And I wonder if she notices my fingers are crossed. But I don't think she does because she smiles and says, "I've got purple jeans and a purple T-shirt. Will that be OK?"

"Perfect," I tell her. "See you there, and don't be late. Community hall, this Saturday, seven o'clock."

And I feel much better and Frankie sighs and says, "You're too soft, Minnie. But please, PLEASE don't invite Trevor."

"I won't," I giggle. "Tulip and Tiffany are more than enough."

And the bell goes for the end of day and I have to tell Mr Impey my numbers. And when everyone has gone, except me and Frankie, I say, "Mr Impey, do you know what these numbers are? And why did they bring us peace?"

And Mr Impey says, "I'm glad you're so interested in the Second World War, Minnie!"

And I don't like to tell him that actually I'm not so I smile politely and he writes the numbers on the board and says, "This is a very important date. It's the day the war was finally over."

14 8 1945

"Oh," I smile. "And do you know what this number is?" And I write my birth-date in numbers on the board, and very carefully I study his face, and it looks confused as he says, "I'm afraid you've got me there, Minnie."

"OK," I tell him. "It doesn't matter. See you on Monday." And he doesn't say, "That's your birthday, Minnie," so he is probably, definitely not the riddler.

FRIDAY AFTER SCHOOL

The bus is waiting, and me and Frankie are running, and we're so late all the seats are taken. We have to stand and it's a little bit like a fair ride and we nearly fall over going round the bends. I get off before Frankie and say, "See you tomorrow in your purple dress!" And Frankie waves and I race home and Mum has painted one of my walls, and my room is finally turning purple. But there are no secret hiding places and it doesn't look how I pictured it. So I cross my fingers and hope it'll be better when it's all finished, as I tell Mum about my riddle.

"I know where that statue is!" says Mum. "The one for the soldier. I could take you there after tea if you like."

"Yes please!" I tell her.

And an hour later, after soup and toast I say, "Can we go to the statue now?"

Mum says we can, if Dad will watch Spike, and Dad looks like he's sucked a lemon and grumbles, "Can't I go with Minnie?"

"No," says Mum. "You went yesterday." And Dad agrees to put Spike to bed as long as it's in MY ROOM!!

And twenty minutes later me and Mum have walked past the playing fields and past the shops, and there it is, the statue for the gallant soldier. Only it's not a statue of a man or anything, but a roundish shape which Mum says is Modern Art. And at the bottom, on a brass plaque, it says,

> CORPORAL FRANK
> BOTTOMLEY
> Died gallantly
> for his country

"Bottomley!" I laugh. "That's Trevor's surname. D'you think they might be related?"

"Probably," says Mum. "There's only ever been one family of Bottomleys I'm aware of."

"And that's enough!" I giggle. "Fancy Trevor having a brave relation." And I cannot tell if they look alike because it's just a round shape, but they probably don't because Trevor's as thin as a sweet-eating whisker and if he was going to be

"TREVO

Modern Art he'd just be a stick.

"What does the Ladybird code say?" asks Mum.

"IE," I tell her. "So what does that mean?"

"IE usually means ID EST," she replies, "which in other words means IN OTHER WORDS!"

"So my code is saying IN OTHER WORDS IT'S BOTTOMLEY, i.e. it's Trevor!!"

"Maybe your riddles ARE LOVE letters," laughs Mum, "and Trevor's your secret admirer!"

"Impossible," I tell her. "Trevor is my worst enemy."

"But you said he sat behind you on the bus the other day."

"Only because he had to," I sigh.

"But he pays you lots of attention," giggles Mum. "And that can be a sign of affection."

"More like a sign for detention," I grumble. "Showing off and doing stupid things."

"We'll see," laughs Mum.

But I refuse to discuss it any more, because it is all too spookily scary!

☆　　　☆　　　☆

When we get home the phone is ringing and it's Gran for me and she says, "Have you opened your card

123

from Aunty Valerie yet, dear?"

"No," I tell her. "Frankie says it's unlucky to open a birthday card before your birthday."

"Oh," says Gran. "Because I think there's money in it and money is always boring on birthdays. I was going to offer to babysit Spike so you and Mum could go shopping and buy yourself a proper treat."

"Really?" I squeal. "Then it'd be unlucky of me NOT to open the envelope. And I know just what I am going to buy!"

And I wish her goodnight and run to tell Mum, who says I can open the envelope and inside is £20!

"Can I buy hair straighteners?!" I squeal

"If you like," sighs Mum. "But what about a new nightie? You'll have to give up that Tigger one soon. I know it's your favourite, but really, Minnie, it's much too small. Maybe you could give it to Dot."

And I laugh so loudly I'm sure Aunty Valerie can hear me in France.

"I HATE THAT TIGGER NIGHTIE!" I scream.

But as much as I hate it I have to have

straighteners or I'll never metamorphose in time for my party. And I go to bed and calculate that I have 22 hours left and I record it on my countdown list before feeling for my key, in my only secret hiding place. But my fingers can't find it!

I get out of bed in a humungous panic and lift the mattress and search with the glowing end of my alien pen. And I rummage through sweet wrappers, and Arana's email, and my old riddles which once were special and looked nice and are now crinkly and totally squashed. And there's so much stuff that I think if me and Frankie were the Princess and the Pea, then Frankie would be the Milanese Princess and I'd be the Arthurs Way Pea. I could never be the princess because I have to sleep on so many things and never feel a thing. But thankfully, finally I find my key, and it had wormed its way too far to the middle of the mattress and I return it to the edge and jump back into bed and drum on my wall for Wanda. She jumps up and sugar-snap quietly I whisper, "Pea to Wanda, over and out."

And tonight I dream I am sat on the bus and I huff on the window and a secret message spookily appears...

TB luvs MP

SATURDAY MORNING

Today is going to be my lucky day. Not only is it my party tonight, but me and Mum are out shopping with £20 in my purse!

I'm desperate to get hunting for hair straighteners, but Mum annoyingly has other plans and steers me to a café and says we should treat ourselves to hot chocolates because it will give us time to think. I don't want to think, I want to BUY, but five minutes later we are schlurping mugs of hot chocolate with marshmallows and cream on the top. And I know Mum wants me to think about a nightie, but I'm not giving in and when I have nibbled a blueberry muffin I tell her, "I really want straighteners for my party tonight. It's going to be my best party ever and I need to look totally extra special, and there's only 7 hours to go and my hair's still a tangled mess."

"OK," says Mum. "You win!" And we down our drinks and set off to the biggest shop in town.

I am so excited, and wondering what I'll look like with smooth hair, when Mum's mobile rings and

Dad's on the line. I immediately panic that it's bad news and Spike is unwell and we'll have to go back empty-handed. But Mum is smiling and turns to me and grins, "It's your lucky day, Minnie Minx. Dad says Tiffany has just brought her hair straighteners round for you to borrow!"

"Tiffany did?"

"That's what Dad says. So now you CAN buy that nightie instead!"

And I cannot believe that Tiff would do that, but... "Perhaps Trevor persuaded her, so I'll look nice for HIM!"

"But Trevor isn't coming tonight, is he?"

"Oh, no," I sigh. "I almost forgot. But I do hope my riddles are not from him."

"Let's not let Trevor spoil our day," says Mum, and we head upstairs on the escalator, and I jump off over the top two steps and ... right in front of me ... are the best pyjamas EVER!

And they have spotty ladybirds dotted all over them and the top is a vest and the bottoms are shorts and it's like they've been made just for me! I'm in pyjama heaven when, can you believe it, Mum says there's enough money for the matching slippers! And they're purple satin with tiny red spots from heel to toe and purple satin antennae that are truthfully strands of a tiny bow. I cannot wait to try them on … until I feast my eyes on an absolutely-must-have matching dressing gown, and it's purple satin to match the slippers, and has a ladybird embroidered on a front pocket spilling spots and hearts like red confetti. And I SO want it, and the pocket would make another hiding place for extra small secret things that vanish under mattresses. But I can't afford it with the PJs and slippers, so after buying some *Chocolates* for Gran and Dad, we leave it behind and head home … TO GET READY FOR MY PARTY!!

SATURDAY AFTERNOON

I plug in the straighteners and I can barely wait for them to get hot and I pass the time by looking in the mirror and pulling my hair as straight as I can. But I just look like a pair of curtains that have almost closed across my eyes, so I go back to the straighteners and they're totally ready to straighten it for real. I call Mum and she comes to help and section by section she pulls the straighteners through my curls. It takes ages and my head gets singed, but I just keep thinking it will all be worth it and I can't wait to see what I look like.

Finally Mum's finished and I run to the bathroom and look in the mirror and … I still look like a pair of curtains!

Dad pokes his head round the door and says, "Excuse me, but have you seen my beautiful daughter, only she seems to have gone missing."

"Stop joking," I tell him, "and call Mum."

And Mum sighs, "It's not quite what I imagined, Minnie."

"Nor me," I tell her. "I don't look beautiful, I just look … peculiar."

And I'm so disappointed, because I thought it was going to be the answer to my dreams and metamorphose me and, "Now what?" I sigh.

"I'll spray it," says Mum. "We'll make it damp, and you'll soon be back to your old self."

"But I don't want to be my old self. My old self is a caterpillar and I want to be a butterfly."

"And so you shall be," says Mum. "LEAVE IT TO ME!" And she fetches a spray and douses my hair with a fine mist and soon it is curling and springing again and she pulls it tight and says, "Tonight, Minnie, you're having a bun!"

"I've never had a bun," I sigh.

"I know," says Mum. "But they always look nice. You'll just have to trust me."

So I cross my fingers and sit extra still and I cannot believe it, but Mum is right. My hair looks amazingly special-party nice and the bits that escape look wispy and pretty and it's hard to think that it's actually me staring out of the mirror.

"Thanks, Mum!" I smile. "It looks great."

"And YOU'RE going to be great!" grins Mum. "Now go and get changed."

And I run to my room and my party clothes are hanging up, and I've never tried them on all together before and I can't wait to see what I look like. But first I dust my cheeks with glitter and paint my nails lavender-purple, and I am so excited it is hard to keep my hands steady. Then I pull on my skirt and embroidered top and I'm thinking I cannot believe how nice I look, when Dad shouts, "I'm off to set the disco up. I'll see you in a bit. Don't be late!"

And I shout back, "But why isn't the DJ doing that?"

And Dad pokes his head round my door and says, "BECAUSE I AM THE DJ!"

And I drop my tights and my heart pounds and I slump on my bed squealing, "WHAT D'YOU MEAN?

I thought we were hiring one to make my party special?!"

"We're hiring the EQUIPMENT," laughs Dad. "...The disco and dry ice and bubble machine. But I'm going to be the DJ."

"But you don't know how to!" I cry.

"I'll learn," he smiles.

"But you haven't got time! And you can't work a bubble machine. And you DEFINITELY don't know anything about music!"

"Of course I do! I like Tom Jones."

"But I don't! You're going to be dreadful and tell terrible jokes and everyone will laugh, and not because your jokes are funny, but because I told them I was getting a proper DJ and instead I've got my dad in purple tights."

And I glare at him through my teary eyes, and, as well as the tights, he's in a purple vest and purple jester's hat with bells dangling from five points.

"Don't worry, it'll all be fine," he grins, as he disappears out of the door.

But how can it be fine when he looks like that!!

"It won't," I shout after him. "And the music's the most important bit!"

"Minnie," sighs Mum, "Dad's only trying to help. And your guests are the most important bit."

"Not when they include the bossiest girl on the planet, Tiff, and my cling-on secret-stealing cousin Dot, and her telltale, knicker-fiddling friend, Tulip! And I've planned this party for so long, and Frankie's planned it with me and made such a good list, and it was supposed to be the best party ever and now it's all going totally wrong! TOTALLY PURPLE-PARTY-RUINED WRONG!!"

"No, it's not," says Mum. "Dad and I have been planning too, and done lots of work to make your party special. So please don't worry. It'll all be OK."

But she doesn't understand what it's like to be me and be wanting something so badly. So I race to the phone and ring Frankie and blurt out everything between my sobs.

"And it's probably because I opened a birthday card," I tell her. "You said it'd be unlucky."

"Don't worry," says Frankie. "Leave it to me."

"But what can YOU do?"

"Lots, Minnie! Trust me. Remember there're things you don't know about yet."

"But what things?!" I sob.

"I'll tell you later, but I need to go NOW if my plan's going to work." And before I can ask her WHAT PLAN? she's put down the phone and gone.

"She says she can fix it," I tell Mum.

"That's good."

But of course it's not good and I know that Frankie is great at ideas, but it will take a miracle to put this right. And miracles don't happen in Arthurs Way.

I'm in floods of tears as I pull on my tights with the silver hearts, and shiny purple pump shoes, and Mum wipes my face and re-applies my glitter and says, "We're leaving in ten minutes!"

"I'm not going," I mumble.

"Of course you are," says Mum. "You look like a Princess."

But what's the point in being a Princess when the King's a jester in a purple-dyed vest and your only Prince Charming is Trevor?

SATURDAY NIGHT

Mum is in a purple dress and Spike is in a purple rabbit suit and we lock up the flat and I drag my heels all the way to my party. When we get to the hall I refuse to go in, but Mum says I have to or she'll get Dad to carry me in. I shuffle in backwards, so I don't have to look, and Frankie is calling, but I just ignore her as it's bound to be bad news. Tulip has probably eaten all the food, and Dot has probably been sick in the crisps, and Tiffany will have arranged for me to sit next to Daniel Jackman, and the whole school will be here and they won't be in purple because Dot will have said it doesn't matter. And I close my eyes and put my hands over my ears.

"What are you doing, Poodle Noodle?" laughs Frankie, and irritatingly I can still hear her because my fingers don't work and there's no music deafening her out so she hasn't managed to find a DJ.

"Don't be silly," she says. And she twizzles me round and pushes me forward and, when she stops, the music starts and I open my eyes and...

Minnie Piper

♪ …it isn't Dad behind the disco, but NERO MINELLI! Frankie's dreamy older brother!!

And Frankie is grinning from ear to ear. And I say, "I can't believe you got Nero to be the DJ!"

"I know," giggles Frankie. "As much as he smells, he knows his music."

"But how did you organize it all so quickly?"

"I started planning it on Tuesday," she grins, "just in case. Over Tuesday's breakfast my dad let slip that YOUR dad was the DJ and I knew you'd be upset, so I bribed Nero by doing his share of the washing-up and buying him a big bar of chocolate."

"But you hate washing-up!"

"I know," she laughs, "but I've been planning this party more than you have! I thought ages ago that the theme should be purple and so the list we made the other night – I'd already done it two weeks ago and given it to your mum!"

"I thought she didn't seem surprised!" I laugh. "So are there more things I still don't know about?"

"Maybe," grins Frankie.

And I know she'll never tell me so I say, "What if I hadn't wanted a purple party?!"

"But you always want absolutely EVERYTHING PURPLE!"

"Oh, yes," I smile. And she really does know just what I'm thinking and she truthfully is my secret twin and my best-ever friend.

THE BEST PARTY EVER

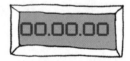

Nero blasts the music out and I look up and Mum has covered the hall ceiling with hundreds and hundreds of purple streamers and fat, shiny purple balloons. And the tables are positioned just like Frankie planned and there are four chairs to each and they are filled with purple beakers and purple lemonade and purple plates and purple bowls.

And across the back wall is a ginormous table with no chairs, but piles and piles of yummy food! Purple-iced cakes and butterfly-shaped sandwiches and pizzas and sausages and bowls and bowls of pickled onion crisps, which Mum says are a treat for the boys as they're not so keen on fairy cakes.

And the doors fly open, and I panic the whole school will come bursting through them, but it's only Class Chickenpox and all of them are in purple clothes.

138

Kevin Little is a purple pirate and looks nearly as good as Johnny Depp, and Daniel Jackman is in a purple bow tie and looks a geek, and Delilah and Tallulah look exactly the same because both are wearing a purple hair bobble. And Jasen is a purple stick of rock and Abhi's in purple, fluffy slippers and Tiffany is in her jeans and T-shirt.

Dot and Tulip are both dressed in matching pink tutus and are swirling about like Sugarplum Fairies. Dot waves, but Tulip immediately heads for the cakes and, when she's found a plateful that tickles her fancy, she grabs the whole lot! And after she's stuffed one into her mouth she grasps Dot and they both hide beneath the table.

"Let's hope they stay there!" laughs Frankie.

And Frankie is in the best dress ever and looks like a pop star. And the top of the dress has a halter-neck and ties at the back and it sparkles with sequins. And in her hair she has purple glitter just like on my cheeks. "I wish I'd thought of that," she says, as she admires my make-up and purple nails. "And I love your hair, Minnie. And your clothes. Even Ruth would be jealous!"

And Mum says, "Is everything OK, Minnie?"

"Perfect," I tell her. "And I'm sorry I got cross, and thanks for making it just how I planned it."

"You're welcome," she smiles. "Are you nearly ready for the dancing competition? I thought it'd be a good way to get everyone mixing."

"OK," I grin, and two seconds later Nero is announcing it over the microphone and he sounds so much dreamier than any DJ on any planet.

"Look out for Tiff," warns Frankie. And talk-of-the-devil, she totters across the floor in her high heels, to make sure she gets right to the front. And Mum and

Dad are judging, and they're at the front, but we don't worry because Tiffany can barely walk, let alone dance. But then she starts moving in time with the music and she is actually a twirlingly-brilliant dancer! And Dot and Tulip come out from the table and spin so fast that I think they'll be sick. And Mum has sprinkled purple confetti all over the floor, and it scuffs up as we all dance and even the boys join in.

And when the music is over Mum announces that Tiffany's won! I award her a spotty hair bobble, and a matching spotty hairband, and Tiff smiles and says, "Thanks, Minnie."

"Thank YOU!" I tell her. "Thank you for lending me your hair straighteners."

"But you didn't use them."

"I ran out of time," I fib, fingers crossed.

And then Mum announces that she cannot decide between who's second and third as they were truthfully just as good as each other. "And therefore," she says, "they are both second! And they are of course ... Dot and Tulip!" And Dot claps and Tulip feeds Spike a chocolate biscuit and they swirl in their tutus like pink whipped cream and I give them both a pink hairband.

And finally Kevin is appointed third, "For your very impressive pirate break-dancing," says Dad. And Kevin looks worried that he's going to be getting a hairband too, but Mum has got him a gobstopper and he gives us a spin on his back on the floor and the music starts up and Nero blasts us with dry ice.

Everyone is having the best time ever, and even Gran is dancing in a purple frock, and Wanda is spinning and chasing her tail which has a purple bow tied to the tip. Then the music stops and the lights dim lower and Mum and Dad are grinning and holding a giant birthday cake and it's sparkling before me on a silver plate. And it has purple violets scattered on top and eleven fizzing purple candles!

But it has to wait as something else has caught my eye, and I can't help but notice Trevor, who is sneakily peeking through a side door. And for a second I wonder if he truthfully loves me, but in my heart I know he's feeling left out, so I run over and say, "I need someone to eat these crisps."

And Trevor snorts, "All right, but as soon as I've scoffed them I'm off."

"Fine by me," I tell him. And beneath his short trousers he's sporting a pair of purple socks.

Then I run back to my cake and blow out the candles, which are still fizzing, and everyone sings me Happy Birthday. I make a wish and when the lights come back on Nero is no longer behind the disco, but up on-stage and his band is with him as he says, "If you don't mind, Minnie, me and the Spider Tigers would like to do a few numbers." So this is another of Frankie's secret things! I just about manage a squeaky, "Yes," as he hits the drums and Dad hits the switch for the bubble machine. The whole hall fills with bubbles that burst and pop as we jump to catch them.

"Great party," laughs Frankie.

"The best," I tell her, "and I don't want it to ever end."

But it sadly has to and eventually the parents arrive and, as the Spider Tigers twang their final chords, it's time to say goodbye.

One by one everyone goes and Mum pushes Spike home asleep in his buggy, and the only ones left are me, Frankie and Nero. And Dad, of course, who is sweeping the floor.

"Thanks, Nero," I sigh. "You were totally brilliant."

"Cool," he smiles. "I had a blast."

And Frankie giggles, "And it's not over yet! There's one more thing that you don't know. And it arrived this morning through my letterbox. I didn't tell you earlier as I knew you'd think about it all night and wouldn't get on with your party!"

And mind-bogglingly spookily Frankie has got HER VERY OWN RIDDLE! She puts it in my hands, and this is what it says:

The countdown to your best friend's prize

Has finally begun

What has three heads at St Peter's

When all others just have one?

Cast your eyes and look on high

And pray it does not rain,

For if it does I fear alas,

Your clue is down the drain.

Go with her as she searches, and may I suggest another,

I think it also may be wise to take along your brother.

You'll need a pair of shoulders, upon which one of you must stand,

He must be strong, he must agree,

or it won't go as I planned!

"Wow!" I giggle.

"Great," says Nero, pumping his muscles, "you can count me in."

"Don't you mind?" I ask.

"Are you joking, Minnie? This treasure trail sounds crazy."

"But what can we be looking for with three

145

heads?" I panic.

"Creepy!" says Nero.

"Not really," says Frankie. "I've already cracked the Ladybird code and it isn't a three-headed werewolf or anything. It's just a gargoyle! You know – those funny heads round the tops of churches."

"ST PETER'S church!" I cry.

And I tell her about my other riddle, and how the soldier was called Bottomley, and how I'm a bit afraid that the riddle is from Trevor.

"Trevor!" laughs Frankie. "But he's fabaroonily clueless!"

"I know," I sigh. "But what am I to do with Bottomley? Especially IE Bottomley?"

"Perhaps it's from Trevor's dad," says Nero, "and he's called Ivan Egor and that's what IE stands for!"

"Maybe," I sigh. But before I can puzzle anything more it's time to say goodbye.

And in bed that night I can't stop smiling because, not only do I have the best friend ever but, I'm going on a treasure hunt with her dreamy brother!

SUNDAY MORNING

I wake up early on Sunday morning convinced that Frankie is setting the riddles! It is highly suspicious that she has one herself and, now that I think about it, Frankie definitely knows MORSE AND knows I like puzzles. We're meeting at the church at eleven o'clock and when Dad drops me off I tell Frankie what I'm thinking.

"You're mad, Minnie! I'd never have the patience to do all that. Plus, I'm absolutely useless at drawing and if I drew ladybirds they would probably look like spotty dogs."

And I cannot say this isn't true and Nero says, "Hi," and I forget all about it.

It isn't raining and we dryly go through a kissing gate to enter the back of the graveyard. I cross my fingers that Nero won't kiss me (like Dad always does), and I find myself blushing as he snakes through.

Then we tiptoe through the graves and look up and there are gargoyles totally everywhere!

"Ours is the one with three heads," reminds Frankie.

And we split up and take a wall each, and I stretch my neck elastically-long because the gargoyles are just so high. And some are broken and have missing nostrils, but when I get to the end of my wall there is not a three-headed gargoyle in sight. I tiptoe round the corner and Frankie is giggling and Nero is with her and there, above us, is a crazy-eyed, three-headed gargoyle! And he has three hands to match his heads and one of them is picking a nose!

"They must have based it on Trevor!" I laugh.

"It's Tulip, Tiffany AND Trevor!" giggles Frankie.

And there's a drainpipe beneath it, about three

metres high, and Nero plants
his feet on the ground and says,
"Who's climbing up then?"

"Minnie!" cries Frankie. "It's
her clue!"

And she helps me on to Nero's
shoulders, and I'm a bit wobbly, but I
can easily reach inside the top of
the pipe … and fish out
a yellow envelope
that's sunflower-
shaped and says
OPEN SUNDAY !

"Open it!" squeals
Frankie, as I jump to
the ground.

HERE LIES
ELSPE...

Inside, on yellow tissue, are twelve spotty ladybirds.

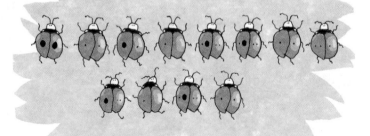

And nearly all the letters are in my name! I know them by heart and, one by one, I call them out and Nero scribbles them on the back of his hand. The first three spell MIN and I am just thinking he's going to have my name tattooed for a day when, irritatingly, the next letter is E and not N. And the E is followed by two L's and in two more letters we have spelt MINELLIS! And I do not know the next letter but the last three are ELI and we all shout together, "MINELLI'S DELI!" And we leg it as fast as we possibly can all the way there!

"Have you got any clues?" I ask Fabio, as he serves us each a pizza.

"Sorry, Minnie," he says, looking totally clueless. "I don't think I have."

And I'm just wondering if I should search the deli

when he pours us a sparkling orange juice, topped off with parasols and strawberries. And as he puts them on the table he says, "I haven't got any clues, but this letter came yesterday and it's very odd because it's addressed to THE FRIEND OF THE MOON."

"That's me!" I cry. "I'm friends with the moon! And her name's Arana and she's my Australian twin!"

"Cool," says Nero. And the envelope is white and moon-shaped and I tear it open and inside, on white tissue, are nine spotty ladybirds!

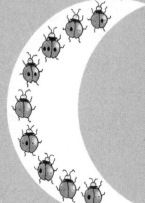

And I'm just trying to puzzle them when Dad arrives to collect me. And he is very jealous of our pizza lunch, as all he had was beans on toast, so Fabio winks and says, "Why don't I give you a little something you can all enjoy at home?"

And he disappears and returns with a white, red and green box and Dad takes it and Fabio says, "It's for tomorrow!"

And I say, "Thanks, Fabio!" and "See you later!" to Frankie and Nero. And Frankie is jumping up and down saying, "Don't forget to ring me when you've cracked the code!"

"I will," I promise. "And next time I see you I'll be eleven!"

"And one year older than me," laughs Frankie.

☆   ★   ☆

When I get home I rush straight to my bedroom and ignore Mum (who's looking suspiciously happy) and grab my MORSE notes and get cracking with the code. I'm getting much quicker, and it doesn't take long to weed out that it spells FLOWER BED but we don't even have a garden and you can't have a FLOWER BED on a balcony.

I phone Frankie and she thinks for a moment before suggesting, "Perhaps it should say

FLOWERPOT! Have you got one of those, Minnie?"

"We've got a window box with geraniums."

"Search that then!" she orders.

And she stays on the phone whilst I go to the balcony and dig in the soil about the geraniums. But apart from dirty fingernails I get absolutely nothing.

I run back to the phone and tell Frankie, and she has no more ideas, unless it's somewhere in the Arthurs Way garden. "But it's just concrete," I tell her. "And the only beds are mattresses thrown out with the rubbish."

"Oh," says Frankie. "I don't know then. Sorry, Minnie."

And I put down the phone and Mum asks what I'm up to, and I tell her about the FL🌼WER BED clue and how I can't find it.

"Hmmm," says Mum, "well there's another sort of bed just waiting to be found! Dad's moved your raft-bed into your new bedroom, which I've finally finished at long last!"

"Really?!" I giggle. And I rush to my room (crossing my fingers that I'm going to love it), and open the door...

Minnie Piper

...and stare at the totally blank, plain walls.

"Da-Dahhh!" sings Dad, as Spike coos.

And all of my furniture has been moved through, but as Mum flops on my raft-bed it looks totally, peculiarly out of place.

"It's brilliant," I lie, fingers still crossed. "It's just what I wanted."

And it IS what I wanted yet now that I have it, it seems yawningly dull. But I cannot tell Mum that I miss my dolphins, because now they are Spike's. So I lie down on top of my bed, and pretend to be overcome with delight.

And it's very strange how I wanted straight hair, and I didn't like that either. And I wish my bed was a flower sort of bed and then it would make my room look nice AND be the answer to my clue. But there's nothing flowery at all about it, even my new butterfly duvet is flowerless, so I bury myself beneath it and shine my alien pen over my star and moon

Da dahh!!

riddles and wonder what they can mean. And it's spookily odd that Frankie had a clue of her own, when it's MY Birthday Treasure Trail. And I think about Corporal Bottomley, and ... suddenly my brain starts to march into action, because he wasn't just called Bottomley... He was Frank Bottomley. IE Frank Bottomley. Or Frank Bottomley IE. OR just FRANK IE! FRANKIE! The clue spells Frankie! And that's why she got her own riddle!

I rush to tell Mum, who's serving up a late tea, and she says I can eat it in my new room. And five minutes later I'm sitting on my duvet and nibbling carrot sticks and tuna salad and suddenly my room's not so bad. It's perfect for my picnic, and even better for clue cracking. I couldn't get FRANKIE surrounded by dolphins, but the plain purple walls have worked their magic! And I stop panicking as at last I know, for a 100%, that I'm not getting LOVE letters from a nose-picking Trevor! And before I can puzzle FLOWERBED I am sweetly fast asleep.

MONDAY AT SCHOOL

MY BIRTHDAY!

It is totally, finally my birthday morning and I wake up in my new room to Mum and Dad shouting, "Happy Birthday, Minnie!" I open my eyes and they're both smiling and Spike is dribbling on to a present. I sit up and take it from him and Mum gives me a butterfly cushion to go behind my back that I swear was not there yesterday. "Where did that come from?" I ask. But Mum and Dad just giggle as they sit down on two ginormous fluffy white beanbags!

"THEY definitely weren't there yesterday!" I exclaim.

"I know," laughs Mum. "You came back too early for me to do the final touches. I had to finish them once you'd gone to bed and Dad sneaked them in, in the night!"

"Mum made them," beams Dad.

"Thanks!" I cry. "They're totally perfect for me and Frankie!"

"Good," says Mum. And she gets up and twizzles her beanbag and there on the back is a big purple **M**. "For Minnie," she smiles, "and sometimes Mum!"

"And mine," laughs Dad, "is F for Frankie. And sometimes Father!" And there on the back is a big pink **F**!

"And the butterfly cushion can be for Dot," says Mum. "Or for sitting up in bed puzzling."

"Or Spike," I giggle. And I give him the cushion and he bounces upon it as I open his present, which is a tiny woodpecker on the top of a pole with a purple feather on top of its head and when you release it, it taps its beak all the way to the bottom. "Thanks, Spike!"

Then I jump out of bed and we go to have breakfast and, as an extra treat, I have scrambled egg and when I have finished Dad gives me a bar of chocolate and we all have a nibble. The post hasn't come, but it's a good job as there's no time to open cards as I have five minutes to get to the bus. I love the beanbags and I sit on the **M** one whilst I pull on my boots, and I just have time to shout bye, before dashing for the bus.

Tiffany says, "Happy Birthday, Minnie," and is properly smiling, and Frankie says, "Sit by the window, *Doodle Noodle*," even though it's not my turn. And I huff on the glass to start a doodle when someone has already beaten me to it! And as if by magic **Happy Birthday Minnie** suddenly appears!

"Thanks, Frankie," I giggle, and I tell her about my room, and how she even has a beanbag all of her own.

"Really?" she sighs. "I can't wait to see it."

"You can tonight if you're still coming for my birthday tea?"

"Try and stop me!" laughs Frankie. "You're new room sounds funky!"

"Mmmm," I mumble. "Actually, it's not that funky. It's not bad either, but it's just a bit boring and purple."

"I thought you liked *purple*!?"

"I do," I sigh. "But..."

And I can't explain, because I'm not ungrateful, and I know Mum has worked especially hard, but it's just ... not me.

☆   ☆   ☆

The bus stops and we've got to school, and we run into class and Mr Impey is not star-jumping but is pretending to be a down-under Australian, and is walking on his hands. "Morning, Chickenpoxers," he smiles. "And I do believe it's someone's birthday!"

And I thought he didn't know!

"Perhaps he IS the riddler!" whispers Frankie.

And he jumps the right way up and says, "Happy Birthday, Minnie. Have you had a nice morning so far?"

"Yes, thank you," I tell him. And, whilst he writes the date on the board, Frankie asks, "Have you found the FL🌼WERBED yet, Minnie? Your new bed isn't flower-shaped, is it?"

"No," I whisper back. "It's just my raft-bed."

"Oh," says Frankie. "What about a flowery duvet? That would make it a FL🌼WERBED."

"Just butterflies," I sigh. "Not a petal in sight."

Then Mr Impey calls our attention and we have to learn about aboriginal art. And I like art and aborigines, but right now I'm more concerned about spots on ladybirds. But totally peculiarly aboriginal paintings are actually made up of nothing but spots.

And Mr Impey has brought in a didgeridoo

and, decorating it from top to bottom, is one long snake. But it isn't painted like normal paintings – it is two twisting strings of white spots. Mr Impey dabs a stick into some paint and dots it over a sheet of card to show us how it's done. Then we have a go and Trevor is excited as we're not using real paint, but runny clay, which is just an artistic word for mud! And we splosh it on to card for a brown background and, whilst it's drying, we crush sticks of white chalk and add it to water and we each have a twiggy stick to dip in and dab. Me and Frankie dab ladybirds, but Trevor has rolled his trouser leg up and muddied himself to his knobbly knee, then dabbed a spotty snake around it so it looks like Mr Impey's didgeridoo! And he loves it so much that he stays like it all through maths and reading.

☆   ☆   ☆

At lunch me and Frankie do not go to the pet shed, but inspect all the flowerbeds around the school. They are not exactly botanically beautiful, but a bit weedy and empty of clues.

"What about your key?" asks Frankie. "Maybe it opens the school shed and we need to get a spade and dig."

"I don't have my key," I sigh. So we nibble our lunch and Dot and Tulip come to see me and sing, "Happy Birthday," and Dot is excited as Mrs Elliot has said she can adopt Matilda, the cutest mouse, and Tulip can adopt Fang, the scariest rat on the planet!

"Oh!" I shudder, and I give them some Twiglets and the bell goes and we all march inside.

Trevor's trouser leg is still rolled up and Mr Impey is so impressed with his dotty snake that he invites him to the front to play his didgeridoo.

"Piece-a' cake," grunts Trevor. But his cheeks balloon and his eyes bulge and his waist button pops off and he nearly loses his trousers round his ankles! Everyone laughs, but then we all have a go, and it truthfully is extremely hard. Mr Impey says we must think of blowing raspberries and I imagine I am blowing mine at Trevor, but all I get is a feeble parp.

Mr Impey is a raspberry-blowing

maestro and he plays us a tune whilst we check our emails from our friends down under. And, whilst Tiff goes first, I retry my Ladybird code. Frankie sees me and whispers, "Well?"

" FL🌸WERBED!" I sigh, as I finish decoding it for the umpteenth time.

And then Tiffany has finished and it's my turn, and **MORSE**-code brilliantly Arana has written her message in dots and dashes! It takes me for ever but finally I crack it and this is what she says:

Dear Minnie,

What is IMPEY? Is it English tucker for going on barbies? Sounds gross. No one here has heard of it, not even Miss Wiley, our teacher. But never mind that — HAPPY BIRT*HDAY puzzling buddie! Xx Arana xx

P.S. Send more riddles soon.

Then I email her back in **MORSE** too and tell her about my Purple Party and searching for gargoyles and how my latest clue is FL🌸WERBED and I don't even have one. And before I know it, it is time to go home.

"See you at half four," I tell Frankie, as I scramble off the bus. And Frankie waves as I race home.

MONDAY AFTER SCHOOL

BUTTERFLIES ON MY BIRTHDAY...

"How was school?" asks Mum.

"Quite good," I smile. "Trevor burst his trousers and I got a secret message from Arana and a gold star from Mr Impey. But I still can't find a FL🌸WERBED."

"Oh," says Mum. "That's a shame. And you've done so well with the other clues."

"Mmmmm," I sigh, as I go to my room to get changed for tea. Gran, Dot and Frankie are coming so I wriggle into my party clothes, lie back on my butterfly duvet and try very hard to wish it had flowers on, and then it would be a flower bed. Butterflies nectarly NEED FLOWERS, but there is not a petal in sight. And then I look up and ... there they are!! Not on my bed but painted on to my ceiling! Flowers everywhere – roses, jasmine and sweet peas.

And, dangling from the flowers, flying on silver threads, are hundreds of butterflies and ladybirds! I'm in butterfly heaven, when Mum sneaks in. "Do you like it?" she grins. "I got the idea at your party after hanging up all those streamers and balloons."

"I love it," I tell her, and I totally mean it! "It's butterfly and ladybird brilliant!"

Then Gran arrives and says, "It's wonderful, dear, though I'm very sorry, I've mislaid your present, Minnie. I put it somewhere secret so that Dot wouldn't find it and now I can't find it either!"

"Don't worry," I tell her, and she sits on my bed, whilst I open my cards, and four of them have £5 in.

"Now you can buy some hair straighteners," laughs Gran. "We didn't have them in my day. I used to iron my hair straight between two sheets of paper, and my best friend Edie, who had straight hair, used to plait hers whilst it was still wet and go to bed with it damp … and when she woke up it was curly!"

And I cannot believe it, but just at that moment Frankie arrives with CURLY HAIR and says, "I've been secretly saving for curling tongs so I can have curly hair like you."

"We're just like Gran and Edie!" I splutter. "Tiff lent me her straighteners before my party but it made me look like a pair of curtains!"

Frankie laughs as she gives me a present, and it's butterfly lights and their wings are made of coloured feathers and totally secretly she whispers, "They'll make your room a bit less boring, Minnie."

"Thanks," I whisper back, "but look up. They'll only make it even better!" And Frankie squeals when she sees the ceiling and says it's so much better than her Jaffa Cake bedroom!

Then Dot and Uncle Jeff arrive and we all sit at the swinging table and gobble jacket potatoes with cheese and beans and when we have finished Dad fetches the gooiest, chocolatiest cake ever and it's the must-open-it-today present from Fabio! And Dad lights the

candles and everybody sings Happy
Birthday, even Spike and Wanda!

Soon we are all so stuffed that our clothes are tight
and, rather than play Twister, all we can manage is
to watch a video. Mum's rented her favourite pirate
film, so I snuggle into my beanbag and stare at the
telly with my head swimming with pirate riddles.

At the end of the film Fabio comes to collect
Frankie and she doesn't want to go. She says it's the
most exciting birthday she's ever had and it isn't even
hers!

Then Dot and Uncle Jeff follow behind her and
it's time for bed and I'm finally allowed to wear my
new pyjamas. Mum says with the £20 I could
always buy the matching dressing gown. I'd
forgotten all about it, yet suddenly I want it more than
anything. "What if they've sold out?" I panic.

"Well…!" giggles Mum. "I took a chance that
you'd get birthday money, and…"

And there in her hands, as if by magic, is the
purple satin dressing gown! And I run to the
bathroom and clean my teeth and slip into my PJs
and wrap myself up in the dressing gown, with the

ladybird-spilling confetti hearts.

And I skip to the kitchen feeling totally special in my matching slippers and Gran claps and says, "You look just like a purple butterfly, dear!" And I flap my imaginary butterfly wings, and wave goodbye to my funky caterpillars as I metamorphically toss them in the bin.

MONDAY NIGHT

MOTHS ON THE MOON

Gran goes home and I can't wait to hop into bed, in my new bedroom, in my new pyjamas, and I twirl there in my satin slippers and open the door, and there … IS A FLOWER BED!!

"When did that happen?!" I squeal.

"Whilst you were watching those swashbuckling pirates," laughs Dad.

And, a bit like the manners-teaching table, my bed is now swinging! Dad and Uncle Jeff have sawn the posts off my raft-bed and attached it to the ceiling by four silver wires. And climbing up the wires are strings of silk flowers!

It looks rosily brilliant, but more importantly it fits my clue and I look on top and dive beneath it, and pull back the quilt and under the pillow, and under the sheet, but there is absolutely no clue anywhere. I cannot believe I've got a flower bed but no answer to my riddle. And absolutely no treasure. I climb into it to decide what to do and Mum says, "Lights out," and I beg her for one more minute, but she completely ignores me and dims the light to no more than a flicker, and ... instead of looking up at butterflies and ladybirds there are moths flitting around my light!

"I thought your lampshade could be the moon," giggles Mum, "and every night the moths will be waiting for your light to be dimmed."

And I cannot believe I have glow-in-the-dark moths! And a paper Arana! "Thanks, Mum!" I gasp. "It's the best bedroom ever, and not just in Arthurs Way, but on the whole of the planet!"

Mum grins and whispers, "Sweet dreams, Minnie."

And I close my eyes, but something odd has happened to my mattress and I cannot sleep and have sweet dreams as I cannot get comfortable.

There's a horrid hard lump where my secrets hide and spookily I begin to think that maybe, now I've metamorphosed, I'm just like the princess in *The Princess and the Pea* and there's something-green-and-round-and-it's-found-on-my-plate-beside-a-kipper-and-two-of-them-are-in-my-slipper beneath my mattress! And I climb out of bed to sneak a peek, but it's not a pea, it's ANOTHER PRESENT!

And it's all wrapped up in spotty red tissue, with a spotty ribbon and a spotty bow, and my heart races as I peep inside and unwrap a wooden box, painted with flowers just like my ceiling! And it's slightly bigger than my Exercise Book but I cannot open it as it's locked shut. I scrabble under my mattress again for my key and, with shaking fingers, I twist it in the lock and the lid flips open!

Mind-bogglingly amazingly the lid is a cupboard for notebooks and pens and the box is made of tiny drawers, and on the front of each is a ladybird! And, ladybird-brilliantly, they spell MINNIE'S SECRETS!

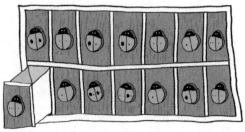

It's totally perfect for keeping things safe and away from snoopers like Dot!

I look up, and Mum and Dad are peeping round my door. "So it WAS you!!" I squeal.

"And Gran," laughs Mum. "I hope you enjoyed it as much as we did. I was a bit worried Dot might tell you about the box because she found out I was painting it."

"So she WAS trying to tell me the truth," I sigh, "and I just didn't listen! But it's the best box ever."

"Dad made it," says Mum.

And Dad blushes and says, "Have you opened the drawers, Minnie?"

"Not yet," I tell him. So I tug at them and tucked

in each is a ladybird chocolate, all wrapped up in red foil, and I have thirteen sitting on my butterfly duvet and we nibble them as I open the last drawer. And there, in the final cubbyhole, is another present, hidden in purple tissue, and it's so small the gift tag is nearly bigger than the gift, and scribbled upon it in Gran's writing it says: Happy Birthday,

"Gran's missing present!" I squeal. "She said she'd put it somewhere secret! So you've ALL been tricking me!" And I tear at the paper and inside is another ladybird. But it isn't red with black spots but totally silver on a silver chain, like a piece of treasure in my treasure chest, and it's totally special ... and totally mine.

"Thanks, Mum. Thanks, Dad. This is the best birthday EVER! Can I just have a moment to ring Gran?"

"In the morning," says Mum. "Right now you need to sleep."

"OK," I sigh. And I put the necklace around my neck and whisper, "Thanks, Gran," and I cross my fingers in the hope she knows I'm thinking of her as my bed transforms to a soft cocoon. Mum and Dad tiptoe out and I drum on my wall for Wanda

173

Wellingtons and Wanda jumps up and licks my face and we both fall fast asleep.

And in my dreams I'm in the garden on my ceiling, and I'm a purple butterfly and Frankie's the leader of the ladybirds and Nero's a moth flying round a paper-light moon. And the moon says, "Good puzzling, buddie. Why not come and join me down under?"

And I snuggle down under ... down under my duvet and my mind swirls as Frankie calls her ladybirds into action and they jiggle to the tune of Happy Birthday and flit from a tulip to a Sugarplum Fairy. And the Sugarplum Fairy sniffs,

"I told you your present was painting, Minnie! Painting flowers on your treasure box!" And, as she twirls the ladybirds swirl and settle on to my flower bed and spottily doodle

Minnie Piper

The first is in 🐞🐞🐞🐞🐞
but actually not
in 🐞🐞🐞🐞🐞🐞 or 🐞🐞🐞🐞🐞,
or 🐞🐞🐞

The second you peek through
and blink in a trice
and is found in 🐞🐞🐞🐞🐞🐞🐞
peculiarly twice
The third and the fourth
are found after 🐞
or in the middle of 🐞🐞🐞🐞🐞🐞
is where they can be
The fifth's in 🐞🐞🐞🐞🐞🐞
but not in 🐞🐞🐞🐞
though 🐞🐞🐞🐞🐞🐞🐞 and
🐞🐞🐞🐞🐞🐞🐞🐞 both have it in!

The last is in 🐞🐞🐞🐞 and
🐞🐞🐞🐞🐞🐞🐞 and 🐞🐞🐞🐞🐞🐞
and 🐞🐞🐞🐞 and 🐞🐞🐞🐞🐞
and 🐞🐞🐞🐞🐞 and 🐞🐞🐞🐞

Put them together
and what have you got?
A 🐞🐞🐞🐞🐞🐞 that's totally
BRILLIANT that's what!